Pr

Simone

I woke up tied to a bedpost by every limb. I was bound at the wrists and ankles so tight that every movement hurt. Through grogginess, the events from the night before began to slowly come back to me.

I came to in the trunk of a car. It was dark and loud. Music was coming through the speaker next to me. I tried to move, but my ankles and wrists were bound. Even as I thought back to it, I began to tear up as I remembered the car slowing down and parking. Then the trunk opened a few minutes later.

At first, I couldn't see who opened the trunk. The sun was shining so bright that it was blinding me. But as he bent down to get me out of the trunk, Jimmy's face was revealed to me. Despite being bound by the ankles and wrists, I tried to kick and punch. Despite my mouth being covered by duct tape, I screamed as loud as I could.

We were in the back of a two flat. There was no backyard. We were in a parking lot. Behind us was a hill. On top of the hill were train tracks. Just as he began to carry me towards the door, a Metra train began to rumble by.

It was hard for him to unlock the door with me in his arms. But he managed to do so, despite me squirming to get free. Once inside the hallway, he dropped me on the floor and dragged me past a washer and dryer. The skin on my back painfully chafed from rug burn. He hurriedly opened another door and practically threw me into the apartment. It smelled like cigarette smoke. The living room was furnished with only a sofa and television that sat on the floor. It was worse than any trap house that Omari owned. Even the bed that he flung me on when we reached the bedroom was a pissy-stank mattress on a rusty metal bed frame.

"This time, I am going to make sure I kill you," was what he said to me as he began to tie me to the bed. "But first, we're going to have some fun."

Every time I attempted to fight, he violently hit me in any organ closest to him. I regurgitated when he would pound me in my stomach. I was forced to swallow my vomit before I choked on it because the duct tape was holding my mouth closed.

With a pair of scissors, he cut my clothes from my body. I lay shivering as he removed my top, bra and jogging suit. He actually showed signs of lust at the sight of my nakedness, and I cringed. I couldn't do anything as he lay on top of me. It burned as he penetrated me. I was as dry as the Sahara Desert. The friction was threatening to start a fire.

He raped me all night. He would ejaculate and leave the room with no words. I knew that he was intent on killing me since he used no protection while depositing copious amounts of his semen inside of me. Then he would return after an hour or two with his hard dick again protruding from his cargo pants. And all I could do was cry. I would cry myself to sleep and wake up to him relentlessly penetrating me. As the night wore on, my vagina and its walls began to swell. He would push his way past the swelling with such force that it felt like he was ripping me open. When he was frustrated by my swollen vagina, he used my ass. I screamed at a high pitch, but it was muffled by the duct tape. I began to feel wetness. But I knew that it wasn't my juices. I was sure that it was blood.

I still lay there naked and shivering, wondering when he would return. It scared the shit out of me to think what his next form of torture would be. The air conditioner was on, fighting the stubborn ninety-degree summer air. Yet, I was so cold that the goose bumps on my skin were creating mountains. My tears dried and froze every time they fell from my eyes. I could hear him outside of the closed door. The television was on. I could smell cigarette smoke. I could hear movement about the apartment. But he never said a word.

That is until the door finally slowly creaked open. There he stood. I kept thinking that this is the same man that I, along with Tammy, hung out with countless times. This was the same man that begged me to tell him where she was hiding. When I told him, it was out of jealousy. He knew that I killed the love of his life, and he was pissed that I'd taken her from him. When I saw the knife in his hand, I pissed myself. Yet, it was so cold that the warmth of the urine felt good as it slid down my legs.

My life was over, and I knew it. Honestly, I couldn't even ask God why. I was reaping what I had sown. I deserved death because I'd sown so much death during my life. For years, I'd lied, manipulated, and terrorized. I lay there with bulging eyes, staring at Jimmy's knife, not even attempting to beg for a speedy death. As thoughts of my treacherous past blurred my vision, I knew that I didn't deserve the easy way out.

For so long, I had suppressed the events of my past that made me the woman that I became. Yet as I faced death, those events came to mind...

JESSICA WATKINS PRESENTS

The Simone Campbell Story

Secrets of a Side Bitch

by JESSICA WATKINS

Chapter One

Simone

It was a fall day in September 1999. The fall quarter had recently started. I was a junior at Kenwood High School, which was walking distance from the home that I lived in with my mother in the Hyde Park neighborhood of Chicago, Illinois.

I should have been doing my social studies homework. It was only the second week of school, and yet Mr. O'Neal had thought it necessary to assign a ten page paper on Brown vs. The Board of Education that would be twenty percent of our grade.

The fuck?

I wasn't on that. I was in my room, which was custom painted purple, with my stereo system bumping 702. I was standing in front of my walk-in closet trying to find something to wear to school the next day. I needed to look cute for my man.

Chapter One

Simone

It was a fall day in September 1999. The fall quarter had recently started. I was a junior at Kenwood High School, which was walking distance from the home that I lived in with my mother in the Hyde Park neighborhood of Chicago, Illinois.

I should have been doing my social studies homework. It was only the second week of school, and yet Mr. O'Neal had thought it necessary to assign a ten page paper on Brown vs. The Board of Education that would be twenty percent of our grade.

The fuck?

I wasn't on that. I was in my room, which was custom painted purple, with my stereo system bumping 702. I was standing in front of my walk-in closet trying to find something to wear to school the next day. I needed to look cute for my man.

♫ See, he's my property,

And any girl that touches,

I might just call your bluff,

'Cuz I don't give a...

Who are you to call my cell?

Oh, I'm gonna wish you well,

'Cuz any girl that tried has failed ♫

"Ayyye! Where my girls at? From the front to back! Well, is you feeling that?!"

I was feeling that song! My man was indeed my property. Finally, I wasn't a virgin anymore. I had sex for the first time that summer. I went from being a virgin and never getting the right boy to pay attention to me, to having a *man* that couldn't get enough of me. And he was so sexy! Unlike the boys in school and in the neighborhood, my man was grown, had money, and was fine, with his tall, chocolate, thick self. It was hard for me to see my man during the summer, but now that school had started, we were going to be able to see each other a lot more since I had off campus lunch. We had only managed to spend time together a few times over the summer, but I knew that quality time would increase now that we were going to officially be a couple.

I was jammin' while looking through the fresh gear that my mother bought me for the new school year. Back then, I wasn't impressed by Chanel or Gucci. My mother had captured my heart with Akoo, Ecko, and Fubu. Baby Phat had just hit the scene, and if you didn't have that cat on your jeans, you were lame as hell. The floor of my closet was lined with Jordans and Timberlands. My mother always spoiled me. She was a Charge Nurse in the Emergency Room at the University of Chicago. She was one of the very few Black nurse managers at the University of Chicago at the time. Though she was a nurse with a very busy schedule, she always had time for me. She never missed a report card pick up, award ceremony or parent-teacher day.

I'd picked out my outfit for the next day: Baby Phat denim skirt with the jacket to match, and signature Baby Phat tee to rock underneath. Back then, there was no exclusive virgin hair to sew in your head. I had shoulder length hair that my mom had allowed me to get dyed brown with blonde streaks and some Milky Way tracks added in the back for length before school started.

I sat at my vanity, wrapping my hair, when I suddenly heard my mom's best friend, Faye, screaming over 702.

"Where is she?! Move out of my way, Cecily!"

I started to freak out. My heart dropped to the pit of my stomach. My joyful mood was replaced with terror and nervousness.

"Shit," escaped my glossed lips frantically as I raced towards my bedroom door to lock it. Then I turned the radio down so that I could hear what was being said.

I could hear my mother yelling. "Don't come in my house clowning! What is wrong with you, Faye?!"

"I want to talk to your fucking daughter... NOW!"

"Well... Why? What's wrong?!"

"You don't know why?! I swear to *God*...," Faye literally growled. "... You better *not* know why, or else I'm beating your ass too!!"

"Faye!" my mother shot back offensively.

I had the bubble guts as I leaned against my bedroom door with my ear to it. I knew that my mother was confused. She and Faye had been friends since they were growing up in the Jeffery Manor. Their mothers were neighbors and friends, so my mother and Faye literally grew up like sisters. When my mother moved out to attend college at Florida State University, Faye was forced to stay in Chicago because she was pregnant. My mother became a nurse, while Faye got married and had four kids that were like cousins to me. My mother got pregnant with me during a trip back home during Thanksgiving break of her freshmen year. Yet, after giving birth to me, my grandparents raised me for years as my mother completed nursing school and then her Bachelor's. Even Faye had helped my grandparents. She often picked me up on the weekends so that I could spend time with her and her kids. By the time my mother finished her Bachelor's, she was ready to raise me on her own as she went to graduate school.

"Move, Cecily!" I could hear Cecily threatening. "Don't make me put my hands on you!"

My mother begged her. "Just tell me what's wrong!"

"This is your problem! You're always protecting that little bitch!"

I could hear the lump in Faye's throat. My mother was no fighter. Though raised in Jeffery Manor, Faye was always way more hood than my mother, who'd lost her street sense as she rubbed elbows with fellow intellects at Florida State University and the University of Chicago. Faye knew that it would take little effort to fuck my mother up to get to me—the person who she really wanted to beat the shit out of.

And, I guess, that's what she did. Suddenly, I heard a commotion and loud thuds. I heard grunts as they wrestled with each other. Then I heard quick and heavy footsteps coming down the hall, right before my door began to rattle from being hit so hard.

"Open this motherfuckin' door, bitch!"

It sounded like she was kicking the door, attempting to break it down. I tried to think fast, but my brain was scrambled with fear and anxiety.

Finally, I decided to just open the door and play stupid.

My hand was trembling as it turned the knob, but I appeared cool and collected on the outside.

"Hey, Auntie Faye." I had the nerve to smile. "What's up?"

She had obviously come for a fight. She wore gym shoes and sweats. Her long hair was pulled back into a ponytail. The anger on her face made her look like a pit bull.

She smacked the shit out of me!

"Bitch! How could you?!" I could hear her scolding me as the blow knocked me off balance, causing me to fall and land on the carpet while holding the side of my face. "I practically raised you!"

"Get your hands off of her!" My mother appeared in the doorway looking frazzled. Her black natural bob was all over her head. Her brown skin was red with anger. Her eyes looked at me, full of fear of what I could have possibly done, while she held her robe closed.

"No, Cecily! Somebody needs to put hands on this bitch! I told you she was fuckin'!"

I cautiously slid away from her. I crawled towards the radiator and sat up against it, all while avoiding my mother's eyes.

"What? Fucking? What are you talking about?" My mother's questions were full of confusion but, as always, she had my back. "And if she is, what does it have to do with you? Did Reggie claim he was having sex with my daughter?"

Reggie was Auntie Faye's oldest child. He was eighteen and pretty cute, but he always looked at me like a sister or cousin. He wasn't who had found interest in me.

Faye knew damn well who had. Her eyes told it all, as she looked at me with tears pooling in her hazel eyes. She wore contacts, but you would have thought that her eyes were real since her skin was so light and her natural, bone straight hair was so long.

Her chuckle was almost demonic as she addressed my mother's questions. "No, Reggie didn't claim he was sleeping with her. My *husband* confessed to sleeping with her when I found *this* in his pocket while I was doing laundry!"

I went from scared to pissed as Faye took the folded up piece of notebook paper out of her pocket. I wasn't ashamed of what I had written. I just didn't want Faye and my mother reading intimate words between me and my man. I'd slipped the note to her husband, Antwon, while my mother and I were at their home in Tinley Park visiting last weekend. He hadn't been answering my calls for a week, so I slipped him the note. Just like I thought, he called and promised to come see me one day this week during my lunch hour.

"Uncle Twon" and I started messing around after he and Auntie Faye hosted a 4th of July party. I'd spent the night, as usual. Faye was passed out from one too many drinks. Their three youngest kids were fast asleep, and Reggie had left with his girlfriend. Though still tipsy, Twon was in the kitchen attempting to clean up the mess. I was still up and offered to help. I'd always had a crush on him. He was sexy as hell. He was only about 5'10", but he had this medium build that was chiseled with muscles that looked strong enough to knock a nigga out. He had a caramel complexion with the biggest, prettiest lips that I'd ever seen on a man. He stayed fly in Sean John, Fubu, and Enyce. Even his teeth were perfectly white, and his soft brown eyes had the nerve to sparkle when he smiled, revealing deep, crater-like dimples.

He was fine.

The older I got, the more I fantasized about him being my first, falling in love with me, and leaving Faye. I had never caught him looking at me in any way more than his wife's best friend's daughter, though. However, at two in the morning, as I moved about the kitchen in those shorts, I knew he was fighting to look.

I should have felt bad for coming on to him and practically begging him to let me pleasure him orally. I was just ready to feel what all of my friends were talking about and make my dreams come true. I was tired of being the only girl with no boyfriend whose cherry hadn't been popped. Plus, I knew that Twon wasn't shit anyway. He'd been caught cheating on Faye so many times.

"You're too young, baby," was his only excuse.

"No, I'm not," I practically purred as I kneeled down before him and looked up into his slanted romantic eyes submissively. "I won't tell. I promise."

His common sense left out of the patio doors as I caressed his dick that was actually already hard in his basketball shorts.

An hour later, I had convinced him to make me a woman.

After that, it had only happened a few more times; usually late at night when I would spend the night at Faye's, hoping that he would take advantage of me. That was the only time that I could see him. He would tell me that any other time or place was too risky. I had a PrimeCo phone that I used to call him as anonymous to talk to him. Sometimes I managed to talk to him, and sometimes I didn't.

Now that school had started, it was on. I had a lot more free time away from my mother and Faye, so he could see me whenever he wanted.

I wanted to take the note from Faye's hands and run from the house as she handed it to my mother. Those words were intimate and for my man's eyes only. My heart beat hard and fast as I watched my mother unfold it and read it.

As she read each word, the seconds crawled by like decades. Her eyes bulged as each second passed. "Simone!" she gasped. "You're pregnant?!"

"By my husband!" Faye boomed through gritted teeth, as she glared at me.

"Is this true, Simone?"

Before I could confront my mother's fear, Faye smacked her lips and rolled her eyes. "Yes, it's true," she told my mother. "Don't be naive, Cecily. It's right there in black and white. Her fast ass slept with my husband. Now she is professing her love to him as if he would really want to be with her."

When she looked down at me, like she was better than me, like her husband wouldn't really want me, I poked my chest out with confidence. "He does want to be with me, *obviously*."

As her eyes bucked, my mother immediately reached for Faye to stop her from approaching me, as she wanted to. "Faye…"

She swung around, and my mother instantly took a defensive stance against her.

"Don't say my name like that! Like I'm wrong!" Faye shouted. "You read that letter! She's pregnant! She wants to be with my husband! She thinks she loves him! She's crazy!"

"I do love him!" I shouted.

Faye looked at me like I was a pathetic fool, but my mother ignored me and turned her attention to Faye.

18

"Obviously, he put this in her head! Obviously, his grown ass is playing with her head…"

"And obviously her hot ass needs to be checked!" Faye snapped as she attempted to barge towards me. "You need to stop drinking long enough to watch her pussy!"

My mother rushed in front of her to stop her. "And if you don't get the fuck out of my house, I will file a statutory rape charge against your husband. Your husband ain't been shit since you married him. He's been fucking other women more than he has ever fucked you." Those words were so shocking to Faye that all fight left her. "Be mad that you have never been able to please your husband enough to keep his dick out of other women! Be mad at yourself! Now get out before I call the police on your ass too!"

Those words crushed Faye. Years of friendship had been ruined in that moment. She stood there a broken woman. She was no longer pissed off and ready to attack. She was heartbroken and worn out.

Cecily

Admittedly, I was scared as Faye walked by me. Though my harsh words had smacked all fight from her, she had the potential to explode at any moment. She knocked me down a few moments earlier just to get to Simone's room. In over thirty-five years of knowing each other, she had never laid a hand on me.

However, she walked by without another word or another attack. It broke my heart that I had hurt her, but there was no way that she was going to stand in my house and act like this was all Simone's fault. Twon was a hoe; he always had been and always would be.

When I heard the front door close, I finally relaxed a little. Simone sat on the floor, avoiding my eyes. I fought tears as I went to secure the front door.

Back in her room, I knelt down and sat beside her. I was shocked that there was no shame or tears of embarrassment. Her face was proud and assured.

"Are you really pregnant?"

"Yea."

"When was your last period?"

"August 19th."

I hid the relief as I told her, "You can't have this baby, Simone."

She couldn't. I was a Charge Nurse. All I did all day was take care of sick babies and pregnant women. However, as many teenagers had begun to have babies for practice, I'd watched so many little girls ruin their lives purely with the hopes of keeping the man that had spilled his seed inside of her.

It never worked.

It hadn't even worked for me.

Instantly, Simone panicked. "Why not, Mama?!"

"Because you are not having a child by some thirty-eight year old man!"

"You can't make that decision for me! That's up to me and Twon!"

That made me sick to my stomach. Her naiveté was scary. "Are you serious? It's up to you and Twon?"

She insisted, "Yea."

"Sweetie, he doesn't want that baby just like he doesn't want you."

"You don't know that, Mama!"

I didn't know what to do. She was sixteen and open. She actually thought that she was in love. I had been there a time or two. I couldn't act like I didn't relate to her stupidity. I remembered my first love and how I had been a fool for him for so many years. I sat there, cursing Twon's existence for playing with my child's immaturity.

When she saw how serious I was about her not keeping the baby, *that* is when she cried. "Mama, please…" Her words trailed off and were replaced with sobs.

I would have felt sorry for her if she really wanted this child, but I knew that wasn't the case.

She wanted Twon. She thought that this baby would keep her in his life.

I just put my arm around her and let her cry. There was nothing else that I could do to soothe her sixteen-year-old heart. I didn't know what to say to make it better. I didn't have any advice to give. I couldn't tell her the wiser when I was still playing the fool my damn self.

✳✳✳✳

An hour later, Simone was still crying. I had left her in her bedroom to work through her feelings.

I was in the kitchen pouring another double shot of vodka with the cordless house phone to my ear, waiting for

Derek, Simone's father, to answer the phone. I knew that I shouldn't have been drinking. I would be useless in clinic the next day. But as my habit would have it, I medicated my sadness and heartache with vodka.

I gulped down the double shot and immediately poured another one while still listening to the phone ring.

"Probably laying up under *her*," I muttered as I contemplated hanging up.

Derek was a ladies' man. He stayed under one woman or the other, despite being married. Admittedly, I had been one of those women off and on for over sixteen years.

Derek Campbell grew up in Jeffery Manor, along with me and Faye. He barely noticed me, while I had a crush on him since I was a freshman in high school. He would have been a senior then, but he'd dropped out. He was a drug dealer, as many of the guys in the hood were back then. I was so amazed by him. Visually, he was impeccable. His skin was as dark as night. His height was incomparable, standing at 6'4". I remembered being on the Jeffery bus and riding by his usual spot on Escanaba. He was so fine, as he stood out there– rain, sleet, or snow. For so many summers, I strutted by him hoping to get his attention. But I never did until the Thanksgiving holiday of my first year of nursing school. It was Thanksgiving Day. Dinner was over. Faye and some of our homegirls wanted to go out since it was my first time being back home since school started. We decided to go to the Cotton Club on 17th and Michigan. The bouncer was Faye's cousin, so we were able to get in despite being underage. I couldn't believe it when I saw Derek there. He was buying the entire bar and gorgeous women surrounded him, along with men who looked like money and cocaine.

To this day, I regret ever going to that bar that night. That night, my life changed forever, and I would never mentally be the same.

I couldn't take my eyes off of Derek. When our eyes finally met, he smiled. I fell in love right then. His personality was as cocky as his physique. I was turned on by the fact that his high self-esteem was a challenge to me. Normally, men fell at my feet. I wasn't the most beautiful woman in the world. However, I was tall, slim, and chocolate. I wore long plaits straight to the back. I looked very modelesque back then. That's what Derek told me that night, "You should be a Jet Beauty of Week." He fed me, Faye, and our friends so many drinks that night. I was drunk for the first time in my life. I didn't know how I ended up back at Derek's apartment with his dick inside of me while I howled like a mad woman. He wasn't breaking my virginity, but it felt like it. My parents were so mad at me when I wobbled back into the house the next morning with a hangover. I was hungover from liquor and love.

I love my child, but I could have gone without the years of heartbreak. I hardly heard from Derek again after that night. He was in the streets heavy. I heard from my friends back home that he had a heavy rotation of women as well. But, as I studied at Florida State University, I could not take my mind off of him. Three weeks later, I realized that my period hadn't come on. By the time that I was back home for Christmas break, I was breaking the news to Derek that I was having his baby.

He wasn't happy about it. "You're what?"

We were sitting in his Mercedes-Benz 300D in the driveway of my parents' home on 97th street between Yates and Oglesby. It was the cleanest car I'd ever seen. Back then, if you had a Lexus in the hood, you were rich. My heart was fluttering as I stared at his profile. He wouldn't even look at me. But even the side of his face was so fine that, even in my sadness, I wanted to reach over and kiss him.

"I'm pregnant, Derek."

He adjusted his Calvin Klein sunglasses and then nonchalantly asked, "How far along?"

I stared longingly at the side of his face. I wanted so badly for him to show me an ounce of love. I wanted him to want to be more to me than a hard dick when it was my turn to make him cum.

I muttered, "A few weeks."

"Are you keeping it?"

His voice was so cold; it was much colder than the twenty degree Christmas air that was surrounding the car.

I was heartbroken. Still under the spell of a delusion, I prayed, literally, that this news would make him want to commit to me and be a family.

I winced. The pain was so surreal. He heard it and tried to comfort me. "I'm saying. You're in college. I'm a street nigga. How are we going to raise a baby?"

He was right. A baby didn't fit into that plan. However, back in the eighties, abortions weren't as acceptable as they eventually became. Admittedly, I wanted so badly to have his baby because I wanted him. I was in love. I had no reason to be. He didn't acknowledge me, send me flowers, or even call me on a regular basis. For the next four years, what he did do on a regular was fuck me every time I threw him pussy to get his attention. For four years, I was focused on nursing school and Derek. Though I had given birth to Simone against his will, he continued to fuck me. But he never fell in love or even committed to me. He was a great father. He loved Simone so much, but he never loved me. Parts of me wanted to be so successful to impress Derek. What man wouldn't want a pretty, educated Black nurse on his arm? He was never in my life like I wanted him to be, though. Then he showed up at Simone's four-year birthday party with a wedding ring on. I could have died right then. I couldn't understand why he was willing to wife some chick when he barely paid attention to me. Stupidly, I continued to sleep with Derek off and on during his marriage. It was a rare event that happened during moments of weakness, but I just couldn't help myself.

I dated here and there, but I never married because the love in my heart was so loyal to one man who never acknowledged it. For sixteen years, my heart melted for a man that was cold towards the love that I had for him. For sixteen years, I'd been his booty call.

"Hello?" Derek finally answered. Sixteen years later, the sound of that man's smooth, seductively deep voice made me weak and my pussy quiver.

"Hey. Are you busy? I need to talk to you about Simone."

"I'm having dinner with my wife. But what's up? What did she do now?" Then he huffed.

Derek loved his daughter. He always financially supported her. They spent time together here and there. However, he was so busy fucking every pussy that got wet for him that he wasn't a man in her life. He wasn't there to teach her the ways of a man. For years, I'd been catching Simone in one questionable predicament with a boy after another. She was caught kissing a boy in the boy's bathroom when she was nine years old. She was doing things to get boys' attention outside while she was playing when she was eleven. She had a "boyfriend" when she was six. I'd come home and caught a boy in my house a few times by the time that she was in eighth grade. The girl was always boy crazy. I always felt like if she got that attention from Derek, she would calm down when it came to men in the streets. I grew up with my father. I wanted the same for my daughter. I faulted myself for not ensuring that I provided that for Simone. To make up for it, I gave her anything she wanted.

I sighed and gulped down the rest of the vodka. "She's pregnant."

"Tuh," he grunted. "I knew this day was coming."

I rolled my eyes and bit my tongue. I didn't want to get smart. I didn't want to argue with him. I hated when we did.

"I need you to talk to her, Derek. It's Twon's baby..."

"Who?"

"*Twon*. Faye's husband..."

"The fuck?! That son of a bitch!"

He was so loud that I pulled the phone away from my ear, but I could still hear him cursing and screaming.

"I'm killin' that nigga!"

Derek knew Twon from the neighborhood that we all grew up in. They were never friends, but they knew of one another.

"I'm calling the police on him," I said.

"He deserves an ass whooping, but don't call the police," Derek told me. "He don't deserve a pedophile rap. Simone has always been fast. He wasn't right, but I'm sure she threw it at him."

Again I bit my lip. This is what I meant by him never being there emotionally for her. He was ready to kill Twon, but didn't say one word about putting his foot in Simone's ass.

I could hear Derek fussing over my thoughts. "That girl is so naive."

She was naive. I couldn't blame her, though. The most valuable treasure that a man can give a girl is a piece of his heart. That's all she wanted. I wasn't in a position to judge Simone. I wanted the same.

Chapter Two

Simone

For the next few days, shit hit the fan. My mother was pissed. She masked it by keeping a drink in her hand. I'd heard her having a few drunken conversations with my father, blaming him for what was happening because they weren't together. My mama had been sweating my daddy for years, but he never chose her.

Luckily, my daddy had convinced her not to call the police on Twon. Everyone was into it; Faye and my mother and Twon and my parents. I was at school fighting my own battles as well. Twanya, Faye's daughter that went to Kenwood, had been on my ass for two days, taunting and fighting me. It got so bad that I had to stay home from school for the last two days.

I had been trying to get in touch with Twon, but I wasn't getting an answer. I knew that he was probably getting into it with Faye. But what about me? I needed him because my mother was making me abort our baby. I needed him to let her know how he felt about me so that I could keep our baby.

It was Friday, the day that I was supposed to get the procedure done. I was scheduled to get an abortion at two that afternoon. Since Twon wasn't answering my calls, I snuck out early that morning and took the bus to his house to catch him before he left for work.

I had a lot of nerve, but fuck that. He was *my* man, not Faye's. I had every right to talk to him about our baby.

I knew that it was time for Reggie and Twanya to be gone to school already. As I got off of the bus and walked up the street, a smile spread across my face, knowing that I would finally get a chance to see Twon.

I was listening to my portable CD player. Aaliyah's words were ringing so true.

♫ I don't wanna be...
Be without you, be without you
I don't wanna live...
Live without you, live without you
I don't wanna go...
Go without you, go without you
I don't wanna be alone ♫

I damn sure didn't want to be without Twon, and I didn't have to be any longer. I noticed Twon's red 1999 Chevy Tahoe in the driveway. The memories of the sex we'd had in there put a coy grin on my face as I walked up the steps and rang the doorbell.

I saw Faye's Intrepid too. I wasn't fazed. Like I said, he was my man way more than he was ever hers.

I stuffed my hands into my Phat Farm jacket. It was colder than expected for a September morning. There was a cold front over Chicago that would eventually be gone by Friday. Then we would be back to our normal low sixty-degree September weather.

I could hear the latches unlocking as a harsh wind blew by. "I'm gon' need him to drive me to school, shit," I muttered as I waited for someone to answer the door.

I got excited as I heard the door opening. Finally, I was going to get to be with my man. We could leave and get out of here; me, him and our baby.

However, when our eyes met, he was not wearing the same smile that was on my face. He looked frustrated. He looked beat up too. My father had really done a number on him. He showed up at this very same house two days ago and beat the breaks off of Twon. Then he shot him in the leg, near his groin. It was a through and through shot. My daddy wasn't worried about Twon telling, since Twon didn't want to go to jail for statutory rape.

Despite the black eye, I noticed how comfortable he looked. He was barefoot and bare-chested, wearing only shorts. I thought for sure that he would leave Faye or vice versa, after they found out about my pregnancy, but I guess no such luck.

With disappointment, I looked at him like how dare he still be with her.

"What are you doing here, Simone?"

I ignored his attitude. "Hey. I've been calling you."

His eyes rolled into the back of his head as he coldly said, "You need to leave."

That gave me a feeling that I had never felt before. It also gave me a feeling that I would never forget. At sixteen, I had never had my feelings so hurt by a man in my life. He was looking at me like I was a problem; when the last time that I saw him, he was looking at me like I was his everything.

Again, I ignored his attitude. "I've been calling you. My mama is making me abort the baby."

His mouth opened and closed. He couldn't figure out what to say before heavy footsteps could be heard behind him. "I know good and gawd damn well!!"

Faye popped up behind Twon. She looked like shit. She looked like she hadn't showered since she showed up at my house. Just like on that day, she was mad as hell.

"Get the fuck off my porch, lil' bitch!"

Her mouth flew to the ground when I folded my arms and said, "I'm talking to my *baby's father*."

Twon immediately jumped between the two of us.

Faye threatened me through gritted teeth. "I am going to *kill you*!"

She pushed Twon, in order to push her way outside, and Twon was pushing back. "Faye, calm down!"

They wrestled. Faye was trying to get to me. Twon was holding her back. He held his arms out, gripping the frame of the door tightly in order to hold her back. He looked at me like I had two heads because I just stood there calmly.

"Leave, Simone!" he told me as he struggled with Faye. "Get the fuck out of here!"

"You're not going to take me to school?"

My nerve made Faye livid. "Bitch!"

Again, Twon was fighting hard to keep Faye inside the house.

As he held her back, Twon kept fussing at me. "Would you get the fuck out of here?! Why are you still standing here?"

"I need you to take me to school."

"No, *little girl*," he managed to say as he held Faye back. "I'm not taking you anywhere! Gon'!"

I cocked my head. "Oh, so now it's 'gon'"? Now I'm a little girl?"

He was so caught off guard that he lost his grip. Faye was able to burst by him. As soon as we came into contact, I slipped on the morning dew on the porch and fell.

"Faye!" Twon called out for his wife. He didn't help me. He helped *her* by holding her up to keep her from falling on top of me. "Go in the house."

Faye continued to fight Twon. "No, fuck that!"

"Go in the house! She is a kid!"

"A kid that you were fucking, motherfucker!" Then, it's like all fight left her body. "You know what? I *will* go in the house. And you stay your ass out here with the mess you made."

She managed to wiggle into the house and slam the door before he could stop her. I could hear the latches locking as I stood to my feet.

"You need to leave, Simone."

"Twon…"

"Leave, Simone!"

I jumped at the vehemence in his voice. I cringed when he looked at me like he didn't even know me. Tears started to fall as I said, "But you said you wanted to be with me."

He huffed, looking at me like I was crazy. That was the first time he ever actually looked at me like I was a child. "Are you crazy? I never said that. I can't be with you, Simone. You're sixteen. I'm married."

"But you had sex with me."

"And that's all it was."

"But…"

"GO!" He even grabbed me by the shoulders and began pushing me down the steps. I had to hold on to the railing to keep from falling again. "I don't want you. I never did. I am not going to be with you. You need to kill that baby because I am never talking to you again… Leave!"

That was the first time I ever felt insecurity and self-doubt so deep that it made me sick. He was pushing me away… *me*; the one that he had been having sex with and the one carrying his baby. He pushed me down those steps and didn't even look back. I stared up at him as he banged on the door.

"Baby! Let me in, please! I'm sorry!"

He was begging for her, when he wouldn't even give me a ride. I gave up. I walked away, towards the bus stop, with tears streaming down my face.

As I walked down the street, I hated the way that I felt. I hated how my heart literally broke listening to him profess his love for her. I hated how stupid and tricked I felt. I hated the feeling of rejection because he hadn't chosen me.

I hated that feeling, and, from that day on, I fought that feeling with every man that I gave my heart to.

Cecily

My heart broke when I saw Simone standing at that bus stop with tears running down her face. It was so cold that steam rose from her face as the warm tears flowed.

I blew the horn. Despite the strong winds, she walked so slowly. I could imagine that her feet were heavy with heartbreak. She sounded heartbroken when she called me from a payphone asking for a ride. I'd taken her cell phone as punishment and to keep her from calling Twon. I couldn't believe that she had the audacity to go over to Faye's house. My baby really did think that that man loved her. Just wondering what kind of things he'd said to her while luring her into his bed made me angrily bite my lip as Simone climbed into my Range Rover.

I didn't know what to tell her. I just felt so defeated as I sat there trying to think of what to say. I couldn't even put the truck in drive. How was I to reprimand her for being so stupid, when I was still stupid in my own way? I wasn't so high and mighty that I couldn't understand her naiveté. Little did she know that we women don't start making better decisions regarding men the older we get.

The dumb ass decisions just keep on coming.

"I want my baby, Mama."

"You want *him*, Simone."

In response, she just sobbed and heaved. Her cries sounded like they were saying that I was right.

"I know it hurts, but he doesn't want you, baby. He played you. It's a hard pill to swallow, but he wanted to have sex with you... not be with you."

Her sobs and heaves got harder and louder.

"But you're going to be okay. He won't be the last man to break your heart. You just make sure that next time it doesn't hurt so bad."

She looked at me like she was disappointed. She wanted me to say more. She wanted me to make it better. I wasn't going to lie to her. I wasn't going to make her feel like men were going to cater to her heart and be loyal. She needed to know that loving a man with all of your heart got you nowhere but crying alone with a baby. She wanted to hear that he didn't mean it and that he really did love her. But I wasn't going to lie. Instead, I put the car in drive. Gravel and debris crunched under the tires as I pulled away from the bus stop.

She cried the entire way to Planned Parenthood. I didn't reach over and pat her knee or hug her. I couldn't be there to hug her every time a man made her cry. She needed to know how to make it better on her own. And by the time that we were walking through the doors of the clinic, her face was dry and the tears were gone.

I was finally able to shed my own tears once the nurse called her to the back. Glancing at my phone, more tears fell as I realized that Derek hadn't even called. I wanted him to come along with us, but he felt like this was something that just Simone and I should do together. Still, I was expecting him to at least call. I was hoping that he would so much that I nearly jumped out of my skin when my Nokia rang.

"Hello?"

"Hey, Cecily. How is everything going?"

It wasn't Derek. It was Maurice, a friend and colleague. He was a Radiologist at the University of Chicago. We'd both started our appointments at the same time. We worked closely together in the ER. Since we were two of few Black medical staff, we became friends quickly. Over the years, we'd grown very close. Around that time, the back and forth with Derek was the worst. Maurice was my shoulder to lean on.

However, over the last year, he started to express having more than a platonic interest in me and even falling in love with me. He'd offered to take me on an endless amount of dates. I'd gone a few times to casually hang out with him, but, for me, it was nothing serious. He loved me. He said it more than once. Yet, I wasn't feeling him like he was feeling me. No matter how many times he bought me roses, no matter how long we talked on the phone at night, I did not like him in the same way. I liked him enough to only allow friendship. Therefore, we'd grown very close over the years that he had been working at the University of Chicago. He was there for me emotionally. He even fixed a pipe or two at my house. Since we were so close, I was comfortable telling him about what was going on with Simone.

"It's going okay," I said with a sigh. "She's back there now."

"How is she?"

"Not good, as is to be expected. Not good at all."

"What about her mama?"

"Her mama needs a drink."

"No, you don't."

"Yes, I do. Double shot of vodka, neat."

"How about a glass of wine?"

I rolled my eyes into the back of my head. For years, he, Faye, and Saundra, my other close friend, sounded like parrots. "You need to stop drinking," was what they chanted over and over again. I was a single mother who was also a freaking nurse! I deserved a drink every now and then. Admittedly, I drank heavily. I could drink any man under the table. But when it came to my two jobs—being a mother and a nurse—drinking didn't affect either one. I wasn't an alcoholic.

"How about you get a double shot of me on the phone with you to help you through this?"

There was so much sincerity in his voice that I smiled for the first time since this ordeal began.

As we talked, I wished that it was Derek who was there for me the way that Maurice was, but that was how fate worked. The ones that you crave never want you.

Derek

"Is that Cecily again?"

"Don't worry about it, baby. Don't stop."

I palmed the top of her head and guided her back down towards my lap. When her lips wrapped around my dick, I relaxed. I threw the phone next to me on the couch as I relaxed into my wife's head game.

She was sick with it.

I wanted to be there for Simone. I knew that she needed me. I would have to do that when she wasn't around her mother, though. Every time I tried to spend time with Simone while Cecily was around, Cecily figured out a way to throw the pussy at me. I had caught it a few times since marrying Angela. Every time I did though, Cecily went right back to thinking that I would be with her. After sixteen years, she just hadn't gotten the point.

"Argh, fuck, baby." I bit my lip. I had to fight the urge to cum in her mouth. I wasn't ready yet. I had to hit that pussy first. After twelve years of marriage, that pussy was still tighter than a vice.

Let Cecily tell it, I was a hoe. She thought I had a line of women. But besides hitting her every now and then

44

while making a horrible mistake, I rarely stepped out on my wife.

Cecily couldn't wrap her arrogant head around why I never wanted to be with her. She created this swarm of women around me in her mind to help her deal with it. True, back in the day, I was a ladies' man. What gangsta wasn't? I was moving bricks and women in the eighties. I was a dealer and a pimp. However, by the time the nineties rolled around, I had given it all up. After a scare with death, I left it all behind. I got shot four times during a robbery. By the grace of God, I lived. Because he allowed me to live, I gave up the pimp and dope game. I turned my illegal money into a real estate company that grossed three hundred thousand a year. I bought and flipped houses instead of bricks of cocaine. I also turned my pimpish ways into devotion for my wife, who'd stuck by me through all the bullshit. She was a down ass bitch like no other.

No, I wasn't the most faithful man. However, no woman could claim that she had my heart.

"Get up, baby. Let me taste you."

Angela eagerly stood to her feet. Her 34G titties bounced. Her big, curvaceous hips enticed me as she lay down on the couch. We had never had children. She had ovarian cancer. She fought the disease daily. But since she could never have children, she maintained the body of a woman in her twenties. It was tight and right.

Every time I saw her naked was like seeing her naked for the first time.

At that moment, my mouth watered like I was about to taste her for the first time. I divorced her legs and then dove into her, eating that pussy like a cupcake.

"Shit, Derek! Yes, baby. Suck that pussy."

She was my all you can eat buffet.

Chapter Three

Simone

I huffed as I got DeMarco's voicemail.

"DeMarco, this is Simone. I've called you like three times. Call me back."

Three years after the travesty with Twon, I now had a boyfriend who was my own age. Well, he was slightly older than me and kinda my boyfriend. I was a freshman at UIC. He was a senior.

I lie back in the bed in my room fighting tears. After all these years, I finally had a man that I loved, and now he was playing me.

After Twon, I was obsessed with making that rejected feeling go away. Baby mama, girlfriend, or wife; I didn't care. If I wanted him, I went after him. I wasn't a hoe. It's just that when I saw a man that I wanted, the challenge of getting him away from another woman turned me on. I was intent on showing him how much better than her that I was. His acknowledgment of that was his choice to be with me over her, whether for a night or forever. Single men were easy to conquer. The ego booster of getting another woman's man to choose me was intoxicating. It was the only thing that got my attention and turned me on.

I honestly hadn't fallen in love since Twon, though. There were just a few guys here and there that were hits and misses because eventually their woman or wife found out.

That is until I met DeMarco Steve Johnson, #68 on UIC basketball team, and a draft pick for the NBA. Everyone was hoping that he'd get picked up by the Bulls. However, at 6'5", 250 pounds, I was eager to let him pick *me* up, so I did a few days prior in his dorm room while his roommate and teammate, Cordell Carter, was sleeping across from us.

That was our first time having sex. It wasn't as romantic as I would have liked. However, considering that he was the university's star player, I was just happy that he was finally on top of me.

"Damn, this pussy is tight, baby," he breathed into my ear as he started to ride me. His southern, Houston accent was damn near impossible to understand. "You're a virgin for real."

I rolled my eyes behind his back as I giggled and lustfully whispered a lie. "I told you that you would be the first to get this pussy, baby."

He started to kiss my neck. If felt more like he was just slobbering on it. I cringed, but I didn't complain. I was a freshman in college with the star basketball player's dick in me. I mean, what girl would complain about that?

I was uncomfortable, though. I was smaller back then. I was never hippy. My frame was petite. The most I had going for me were my big breasts. They were 34" DDD's that men drooled over. For years, they were my attention getters. However, the evolution of big booty video models like Melyssa Ford had every man desiring a woman with a fat ass all of a sudden.

DeMarco was so big. His dick was even bigger. With every thrust, I felt like he was stretching my insides. There was no foreplay or tongue kissing to make this more pleasurable. He didn't even suck my nipples to make my pussy wet. He hadn't even bothered to take off his clothes. He still wore the Coogi shirt and jeans that he had on at the party. The jeans were around his knees. He was lodged between me and my Apple Bottom jeans that were still around my ankles. I tried to kick them off so that I could move and make this dick as good for me as he was making this pussy for him.

"Shit, girl. Arrrgh!"

He was so loud that my eyes darted over to Cordell, praying that he hadn't woke up. He was still in a drunken coma. We had all been at a party on campus. After tons of Kappa punch, he was out of there. Me and DeMarco would most likely be too, as soon as he was done.

"You like this dick?"

Again, I rolled my eyes. All of his weight was on top of me, as he gripped my ass with his face buried in my neck and drilled me.

"I love this dick, baby," I crooned as I attempted to kick off my jeans.

I felt them coming off, so I began to feel relief. Now I could actually feel some satisfaction too. But no such luck. By the time I was able to free one leg, this nigga was nutting already.

"Argh! Shit!"

"Ssshhhh!" I pleaded.

"Damn, girl," he breathed heavily.

I was cringing as I could feel his sweat leaking into my pores. Thankfully, he rolled over.

"Woo," he sighed, slapping my bare ass. "That was some good pussy. Thanks."

Thanks? My eyebrows curled with disbelief while I stared at the ceiling.

I started to say something, but I soon felt his hands playing with my pussy. I smiled, grateful that he was into me and ready for round two.

"I gotta get some sleep before practice. I'll holla at you later, lil' mama. Ah ight?"

He was kicking me out! I couldn't even look at him. To show him how stupid I felt would have made me feel even dumber. I swallowed my pride and my broken heart. "Okay, baby."

I sat up, hoping to get my kiss before leaving. But he rolled over, turning his back to me. "Can you lock the door on your way out?"

That was three days ago. I hadn't heard from him since. I lay back in bed with a math book and papers all around me. I couldn't focus on my assignments. Not talking to DeMarco had me spent. I couldn't believe how he had played me that night. I wondered if all his previous sweet nothings and promises were just games to get some. If so, I would be devastated.

As I fought tears, my cell phone rang, displaying DeMarco's name and number. I freaked as I jumped to accept the call.

I tried not to sound so frantic when I answered. "Hello?"

"What up?" he answered coolly.

"H... Hey. What's up, baby?"

He simply repeated himself. "What up?"

I tried to talk over the tension. I smiled, hoping that he could hear it through the phone. "Nothing. I was just calling to see how my man is doing. I haven't talked to you in days. I miss you."

"Your man? I never said that I was your man, Simone."

Truth be told, he hadn't. But I didn't need verbal confirmation to know that he was my man. I was claiming him when I gave him some pussy.

I was fixing my lips to say something flirtatious and charming, but he cut me off. "Aye, I'm getting out of practice. I'll holla at you later."

Before I could say a word, the other end went silent. I looked at the phone with confusion, watching the timer blink to confirm that the call had ended.

I was crushed. I wasn't going to let that stop me, though. The next day was a birthday party for one of the teammates at a frat house. I was sure that DeMarco was going to be there, and I intended to be there too.

Cecily

Saundra and I were at Reese's Lounge on 87th and Honore. Saundra was an ER nurse at University of Chicago as well. Though I was her manager, we had become very close over the years. We were off of work that day, after pulling twelve-hour shifts for four days straight. Strong drinks and orders of Reese's signature, tasty fried chicken were overdue.

Saundra eyed me suspiciously as I sipped the Long Island Iced Tea.

"What?" I asked her with a knowing grin.

"Should you be drinking that?"

I rolled my eyes into the back of my head. "It's fine, Saundra."

It really was. Over the past three years, I had slowed down on drinking.

"I don't drink my emotions anymore," I told Saundra.

"I'm sure you don't. Probably because Maurice is *drankin'* your bath water."

I had to blush.

"Ooooooo!" Saundra squealed. I could hear her over the house music that thundered through the speakers.

Chicago was known for house music and stepper's jams. "I'm so happy you finally gave into Maurice. I love you two as a couple."

I held my hand out to stop her. "Whoa. Hold on. Couple is a stretch."

It really was. I had only given into Maurice's pleas about six months ago. The soberer I was, the more I realized how ridiculous I was being for continuously pushing away a *Radiologist*...a good looking one at that.

"So, y'all ain't a couple?" Saundra asked despite a mouthful of chicken.

I drenched my chicken with mild sauce as I fought more blushing. "We're on our way."

We were on our way. I couldn't deny it. Maurice had been making up for the years that I literally ran away from his love. There had been endless dates, wining and dining, dozens of roses and a few weekend getaways... and he had even started paying my mortgage.

"Please tell me that you've fucked him by now."

Unfortunately, I hadn't. Emotionally, I was happy. But I couldn't deny how I was still emotionally and physically committed to Derek. I knew that once I had sex with Maurice, he would be stuck to me like glue. There was no doubt that Derek would find out that I had a man. Every time I thought of that, it broke my heart and scared me. I had become so comfortable with waiting on Derek, and now there was a chance that we could finally be together.

I didn't want Maurice to fuck that up.

"Not yet."

"Why not?! He is so tall, dark, and *thick*. Girl, his feet are so big. Gots to be a size thirteen. That means his dick is to his knees!"

She laughed at her own raunchiness, as I felt disappointment that I didn't feel any lust towards Maurice of my own. She was right. Maurice was everything physically that any woman could want. As we danced a few times, I felt how impressively sized his dick was as it pressed against my backside.

I should have been as excited to fuck him as Saundra was for me to fuck him. But I wasn't, and I hated it. I hated how I was so transfixed on Derek that I couldn't give not even my body to anyone else.

"Girl, please fuck that man." Saundra gulped down her Jameson while signaling for the bartender to bring her another one. "What's the hold up?"

I rolled my eyes and tried to hide the obvious. When Saundra saw my face, she sighed with disappointment and rolled her eyes.

"You're hesitant because Derek is single again."

She couldn't hide her disgust with my stupidity. I couldn't hide my shame either.

"Are you serious, Cecily?!"

"I love Derek, Saundra. I can't help it."

"Have you slept with him recently?"

When I answered, "no," she let out a sigh of relief.

I hadn't, though it was no choice of my own. Now that Derek was a single man, I didn't know which was more excited—my pussy or my heart. This was my opportunity to get the man and the marriage that I always wanted, but he had yet to take the bait.

However, I told Saundra, "Angela has been dead only three months. I love him, but I am not that desperate."

That was a gawd damn lie. I *was* that desperate. When Angela died three months ago, my heart skipped a beat. The ovarian cancer had spread to her chest a year ago. Derek stayed by her bedside. He was devastated. He was even more distant from me than he was before. We hadn't even had one of our random booty calls in over a year. When Angela lost her battle, Derek was crushed. I totally took it as an opportunity to flirt and get back in.

It wasn't working, but I was confident that it would. I always managed to get him in bed. Getting him to commit was the issue. I had never gotten over him choosing Angela over me. Now that there was no Angela, I had another shot.

Yes, Maurice was good to me. However, I loved Derek. I wanted to be with him. I deserved to be with him. He completed me. Even though I was with a good man, he didn't make my heart melt like Derek did. Derek was a quest that I had yet to conquer. I was intent on conquering him.

I had to.

"You better not," Saundra told me with those judgmental dark brown eyes. She was reading my mind. "That woman just died."

I pretended to pout. "And it is *so* sad."

She shook her head. "You're a bitch."

I unsuccessfully held back a grin. "Anyway, how is Faye?" I didn't really care. We hadn't talked since that whole ordeal with Twon and Simone. A lifetime of friendship was washed away with just a few words. I guess my daughter getting pregnant by her husband and my baby's daddy shooting her husband didn't help matters either. But I had grown used to her absence. I didn't really care that we weren't friends or how she was doing. I was just changing the subject.

Saundra and Faye had become friends through me. They remained friends throughout the years. About four months ago, Twon and Faye got a divorce. Saundra told me that *now* Faye was finally tired of Twon's bullshit.

Of course, Twon wasn't taking it well at all.

"She's as good as to be expected. Twon is acting a fool. He thinks that she left him for another man. I guess he is oblivious to all the shit he's done over the years. Guess he can't fathom the girl just being tired...But don't ask me about Faye to change the fucking subject," she fussed. "You need to leave Derek alone. He's no good for you. He had you drinking and shit. He doesn't want to be with you, Cecily. If he did, he would have committed to you years ago." I waved my hand dismissively and even turned my chair away from her. Yet, she turned me back around and made me face her. "Maurice loves you. You've been single for way too long. It's time for you get married to someone who loves you. *Let Derek go.*"

Chapter Four

Cecily

The next day, I figured that Saundra was right.

I had spent my off day with Maurice since he had the day off too. Initially, we wanted to spend the day in Hyde Park. It was a Saturday in late April. The weather was finally breaking. The icy cold was going away. Finally, some bearable weather was sneaking in. We wanted to walk to Harper Theater and catch a movie. However, Simone was in such a funky mood that I wanted, not only out of the house but also out of Hyde Park. Her boyfriend, DeMarco, wasn't answering her calls, so she was in a bitchy mood.

So instead, Maurice picked me up so that we could have dinner and spend the rest of the night downtown at his condo. I was dressed in a black Donna Karan midi dress when I stepped outside of my house. It was fitted, hugging curves that I'd acquired over the years. I was busty. My hips were wide, which made my waistline appear smaller. I didn't have a six-pack, but I was able to smooth out the pudge with a good pair of Spanx. I didn't have a—what the kids were calling—"phat ass." But it was enough back there to attract the men. I wore my hair in a bun, which brought out the modelesque features in my face that were aging at a slow pace, thank God.

My red matte lips fell open at the sight of Maurice standing on the passenger side of his black Bentley convertible. The passenger side door was open, as he stood holding it with roses in his hands. There were so many roses; I guessed there were more than three dozen. I tried to act nonchalant, but it was such an amazing sight to see. It was something that I had only seen in romantic Lifetime movies.

Chivalry isn't dead, I guess, I thought as I sashayed towards the car. I was trying my best to look sexy while I tried not to fall in the five-inch pumps on my feet.

"Hey, baby," he crooned in his low, bedroom voice as he kissed me. His hand in my lower back brought me closer to him. I felt his erection on the other side of his slacks that he paired with a casual suit jacket and shirt, minus the tie. He was already hard, which sent a chill down my back and a nasty thought through my mind.

"These for me?"

He handed them to me with a smile that was devilish. "No, they are for the most beautiful woman in the world."

Saundra is right, I thought as I took the roses with a smile. *He definitely deserves some pussy.*

"Wow, these are so heavy."

"They should be. That's seventy-two roses in your hands. I picked each one myself. It took me an hour." I was speechless. "Here. Give them to me. I'll put them in the backseat for you."

He helped me into the passenger seat. As he closed my door, I tried to remember the last time I had been treated so nicely. Every time I thought of a time remotely close to this, it was with Maurice. I thought of how I wished that Derek had even the slightest inkling of how to treat me this way. The thought of him made me check my cell phone. Derek still hadn't called back. I didn't want anything when I called while I was getting dressed. I just wanted to hear his voice because I wished that I was getting ready for a date with him. I left him a message telling him that I needed to talk to him about Simone, hoping that that would make him return my call faster. But it hadn't.

Maurice and I went to dinner at Gibsons Steakhouse. I was a nurse that made good money, but I was raised in the hood. Never had I been to Gibsons or had a desire to eat there. Now I knew what I'd been missing. The filet mignon melted in my mouth. The creamed spinach was to die for.

However, as Maurice attempted to make me laugh... as his smooth hand gripped my thigh firmly... I could not take my mind off of Derek. I couldn't stop checking my phone. I couldn't stop the sick feeling in my stomach that made me irate because I wondered who was keeping him from calling me back. I wondered if it was another woman—another woman that he would find more interesting and more compatible than me.

I was so wrapped into my thoughts. I smiled at Maurice, pretending to be listening to every charming and alluring word that he said. But I didn't hear a thing. Not one thing. I was so absorbed into Derek's pure disregard of me that I was pissed by the time that dinner was over.

"Slow down, baby." Maurice held his hand out, interrupting my French kissing of my vodka glass.

I wanted to give him the look of death. I managed to smile. "I can manage, Maurice. I'm not drinking to get drunk."

I was drinking to make that nauseous feeling of defeat go away.

Before Maurice could argue with me, the waiter came with his receipt. With his attention on something else, I snuck and gulped down the rest of the drink.

I managed not to get drunk off of liquor. I was drunk with something else though; hate. No matter how much Ron Isley and Sade that Maurice played as we made our way to his condo, I was steaming on the inside. No matter how much he caressed my thigh, I was drunk with pissivity and hated the audacity of Derek that he never gave me the regard that my heart always, *always* gave him.

I fucked him. Back at his condo, as soon as we walked through the door, I fucked Maurice. It was out of spite. I knew that Derek was somewhere with his dick in some bitch that didn't even love him like I loved him. So as soon as I dropped my purse on his leather sofa, I reached for Maurice's belt.

His eyes bulged. "What are you doing, baby?"

Admittedly, I felt so amateur as I unzipped his pants. It had been so long since I was that close to any dick besides Derek's. "What do you think I'm doing?"

He didn't argue with me. He knew better. For years, he'd chased this pussy, and now I finally was going to let him catch it.

Simone

♫ I need a girl to ride, ride, ride

I need a girl to make my wife

I need a girl who's mine oh mine

I need a girl in my life ♫

Joi rocked awkwardly to the overly loud music as we walked into the frat house. It was so damn loud that I had to scream into her ear.

"I'll be back."

She looked at me like I was crazy. "Where are you going? We just got here."

"I gotta go find DeMarco."

She rolled her eyes into the back of her head. As I walked away from her, I didn't give a fuck what she thought. She assumed we were friends, so she idiotically felt I would actually care about what she thought. We weren't friends in my eyes, though. She was just the only person that I could drag along with me to parties. I would have preferred my cousin, Jasmine, to come with me. She had curves for days and was definitely a nigga magnet.

DeMarco and the team would have definitely flocked around us if she was with me, but she flaked. She was most likely under that nigga she had been glued to for three years.

Therefore, I was stuck with Joi. I didn't have many female friends. Well, none, actually. Since high school, I'd lost one friend after another. Women just didn't like me. That's why I stayed at home instead of going away to school or staying on campus.

Joi was a lame that I became cool with in Speech class the first semester of freshman year. She was such a fucking lame. Even that night, she wasn't rocking any labels. She had on dingy, no-name jeans, a dingy tank, and some Converse sneakers. Her hair wasn't even combed. I couldn't be caught with her. I was looking too fly and on purpose. I had to catch DeMarco's eye, who hadn't called me back from the night before. But, in my Parasuco blue jean mini skirt and belly shirt, I was definitely going to get his attention that night.

It was hard to see. The frat house was dimly lit. Even more, the weed smoke was thick. People were everywhere. The first floor of the frat house was full of drunk UIC students that were clearly too young to be drinking. My mother drank so much when I was younger that I had no interest in the stuff back then.

I didn't see DeMarco anywhere, so I climbed the steps to the second floor. Even the stairs were jam packed. Random hands found their way up my skirt. I smacked them away each time without looking back. I was on a mission. I'd called DeMarco three times that day with no answer.

I was peeking through doors as I walked by. I prayed that I didn't see DeMarco behind any one of them with a chick. That's what happened at these parties—lots of fucking.

In the last bedroom, it wasn't him in the room with some random hoe. It was Cordell getting head from some redhead white girl. DeMarco was sitting on the bed opposite of him, staring at his phone.

They didn't even notice me creep in. The music drowned out my footsteps. They appeared to be too drunk to pay attention anyway.

"You callin' me back?"

When DeMarco looked up, he smiled. His eyes and smile were full of lust. I couldn't have been more excited. His eyes rode low as he said, "What's up, shawty?"

"Hey." I sat beside him, and he immediately put his hand on the warmest part of my thigh.

"You lookin' sexy, shawty."

Damn, that accent was sexy as hell.

"I've been calling you."

"I know. I've been busy with practice." As he talked, his hand went further and further up my leg until it found my lace panties. "I'm sorry, baby."

I was so happy to finally be with him that I let it go. I put my hand on DeMarco's thigh. He'd pushed me away for days, but he didn't push my hand away as it started to caress his dick.

"I miss you," I told him.

"How much?" When he licked his lips, I smiled. Finally, his cold exterior was going away. "Show me."

I wanted nothing more than to be DeMarco's girl. It hurt my feelings when he stopped calling after our first session. I figured that he needed more persuasion. When the bass would momentarily fade, I could vaguely hear the white girl behind me slurping and Cordell moaning. When I stood to my feet, I guess I caught the White girl's attention.

She stopped what she was doing and looked behind her. As I got on my knees and started to unbuckle

DeMarco's pants, she started talking shit. "The fuck? No. This isn't that type of party," she said standing up.

"Hold on, shawty," Cordell called after her, but I could see her storming out of the room out of my peripheral.

"The fuck, man!" Cordell was fussing, but I kept slurping. I could feel DeMarco's hand in my hair, guiding me up and down his dick.

"This is some bullshit," Cordell hissed.

Then all got quiet. I assumed Cordell was leaving out until I felt hands going underneath my skirt. Immediately, I stopped.

"The fuck?!" I looked back at Cordell. He was so into what he was doing that he didn't look up at me. He was holding his dick and dropping to his knees. I looked up at DeMarco for help, but he simply wore the sexiest grin on his face.

"Don't stop, baby," he said in his most tender voice as he ran his fingers through my hair. I was still looking at him curiously. So he got mad. "Why you get down there if you weren't 'bout it?"

I didn't want him to be mad. He saw me contemplating, so he told me, "It's not a big deal. If you wanna fuck me, you'll fuck with us. Just one time. Show me how much you miss me. Show me you're down."

I fell for that shit. Wish I could say that I was drunk, but I was soberer than anyone at the party.

I took DeMarco back into my mouth, as I could feel Cordell penetrating me. In all honesty, it felt so fucking good to have Cordell thrusting inside of me as DeMarco palmed my roots and guided my head. They weren't rough. Cordell's hands were softly on my waist, as he rode me with perfection. He was taking his time in it.

"Damn, this pussy is tight."

Then DeMarco chuckled. "I told you, nigga."

That stroked my ego. I started to rhythmically throw it back as I drenched DeMarco's dick with spit and heard him hiss. "Damn, girl."

I could feel myself getting more and more aroused because I knew that DeMarco was enjoying it.

"That's it, lil' mama," he encouraged me. "Get it."

Listening to his lustful affirmations as Cordell moaned in excitement behind me gave me such a rush. DeMarco's moans were getting so loud that I could start to hear them very well over the music. I could feel the veins of his dick pulsating inside of my mouth. Suddenly, I could feel Cordell pulling me up. As we stood, he caressed my breasts.

I could feel my nipples harden. DeMarco stood as well and began to make circular motions on my clit.

"Mmmm," I moaned.

DeMarco's eyes burned into mine. "You like it, baby?"

I nodded, unable to speak from the sensation of four strong hands all over me.

"I want to feel that pussy. Come here."

He sat back down on the bed as he reached into his pocket. He tore the condom off with his teeth as Cordell continued to play with my nipples. Once the condom was secure, he pulled me on top of him. I straddled him and slid down easily. I couldn't believe how excited I was. I could feel my juices running between my legs. I was even more excited to see the eagerness in DeMarco's eyes.

Cordell climbed into the bed. He stood up in it, holding himself up on the wall. He was also gentle and persuasive when he palmed my head and guided my mouth towards his dick. As I took him in, DeMarco freed one of my breasts and started to suck it. The feeling was indescribable. The orgasm that I could feel coming was more intense than anything I had ever felt before.

Derek

"Why is she calling you at midnight, Derek?"

I snatched my phone back from Patricia. "What are you doing with my phone?"

She was a broad that I knew from back in the day from Jeffery Manor. We used to fuck around when I was in the streets. She was happy to hear from me after Angela died. I needed a fuck buddy, and she was down.

"What are you doing with my phone?"

"It kept ringing while you were in the shower. I couldn't help but look. I wasn't going to answer."

Patricia ignored the way that I was glaring at her. She looked at my chest as she licked her lips. She looked like she wanted to lick me dry and snatch my towel away. No matter how phat that ass was or how good that wet mouth was, I wasn't having it. I was fuming. My wife had only been dead for a few months, and already random ass women were trying to fill her shoes. As soon as the heart monitor stopped, it was like some smoke signal went out to every single...and married...piece of pussy that ever wanted me.

Fucking vultures.

"Are you still sleeping with her?"

My eyes rolled in the back of my head, as I walked over to the other side of the bed. Her eyes followed me, as she lay naked on top of her brown and orange down comforter.

She was so chocolate that she almost blended in. Looking at her perky breasts, even in her late thirties, my heart softened, and my dick hardened.

"Nah, I'm not fucking her, baby," I said. I reached over and squeezed her thigh, which was still sweaty from the hour-long fuck-fest that she suffered through. Angela had become so sick that sex was painful that last year of her life. Then, towards the end, I spent months by her bedside until she passed.

Me and my dick were definitely getting back into the swing of things. Honestly, I didn't want Patricia or the random booty call. I missed the love and comfort of my wife. I had found that in someone else and preferred to be under her. We had grown close during the year of Angela's suffering. She helped me through it. I admittedly fell for her during that time, but she refused to sleep with a married man. Then she refused to be a rebound now that Angela was dead.

So I was stuck fucking randoms like Patricia.

"Then why does she call you all the time?" I would have had some kind of snappy comeback, but as she spoke, she took the Jergens lotion from my hand. Then she laid me down and started to moisturize my skin.

"She's my child's mother. We've known each other since we were kids. She's just checking up on me. She's concerned since Angela passed."

That was a gawd damn lie. Damn near twenty years and Cecily just couldn't let go. Her ego wouldn't let her. She was one of the single pussies that thought it was a free for all when my wife wasn't even cold in the ground yet. Her stalker level went from five to sixty, no sooner than the slow singing and flower bringing ended.

Simone

Over an hour later, I was sweaty, sticky, and pretty sure that there were questionable bodily fluids in my hair. But DeMarco had the most admiring smile on his face that told me it was all worth it.

Even Cordell's world was rocked. It was a small sacrifice for the bigger picture.

"Ah ight, shawty. I'll get up with you." I felt a smack on my ass as I looked up. I was putting my clothes back on. DeMarco and Cordell had easily pulled their jeans up and were walking out.

"DeMarco, baby, wait!"

DeMarco couldn't hear me over *U Don't Have to Call* as it blared through the house's surround sound system while he and Cordell closed the door behind themselves.

I hurriedly stumbled back into my skirt. You would have thought I was tipsy. But the sexual experience that I just had made me a bit dazed. My legs were weak—so weak, that I tripped over my own feet.

"Arrgh!" I shouted as I toppled over. I fell into the nightstand, knocking the lamp and alarm clock down with me as I hit the floor. As I fell, I could feel my arms and legs bumping heavily against various things in the dimly lit room. "Shit!"

My legs were throbbing. My arms were burning. I knew that I had to have a few cuts and bruises, but it was too dark to tell. My eyes burned with tears. I got myself together fast, though, in order to run after DeMarco.

I wiped my face free of tears as I walked out of the room.

"Damn, shawty. You okay?"

I shot a mean mug at whoever the guy was that was asking, and I kept walking.

The hallways were still thick. However, it seemed like in that hour that the atmosphere had changed. Drugs had taken effect. Liquor had kicked in. Movements were slow. Visions were blurry. Pupils were severely dilated. I was probably the only person that was sober. However, I was probably the only person that had done something that one could only blame on the effects of weed and a lot of fucking alcohol.

Back downstairs, I was looking for DeMarco but bumped into Joi. Her glasses were off balance, and her smile was intoxicated.

"Simone! Where you been? I was just looking for you."

"Have you been drinking?" I asked.

She giggled. "Girl, yea. That Beta House juice is *skrooooong*."

I huffed and looked over her. My eyes fell on DeMarco. When I smiled, he didn't.

"What's wrong with you? Have you been crying? Did you know that your arm was bleeding?"

I didn't answer her goofy ass. I was too busy staring at Adina Manning, a cheerleader with the perfect body. She was standing close to DeMarco's chest, facing him with her arms around his waist, swaying to the Mary J. Blige that was now playing.

"Yea, girl. Soon as he came downstairs, he bee-lined towards his bitch." Obviously, Joi saw what I saw. "That's why I've been looking for you. Where you been anyway?"

I looked at her like she had two heads. I tried hard not to vomit as I stomped towards DeMarco. He even tried to act like he didn't see me coming. He put his face into Adina's neck, as they slow danced. That pissed me off even more.

I tapped DeMarco on his shoulder like Adina wasn't standing right there. "Can I talk to you for a minute?"

However, I got her attention as DeMarco attempted to act like I wasn't there. Adina was obviously annoyed, but so was I. It hadn't even been ten minutes since he pulled out of me, and he was just going to ignore me?!

"Baby, why is this basic ass bitch talking to you?"

I can't tell what hurt worse—the fact that she called him baby or that she called me basic.

My eyes squinted with confusion. "Basic?!"

DeMarco totally dismissed me. "Don't worry about her, beau," he said as he frowned at me and waved his hand in my face. The front he put up just because she was standing right there was heart wrenching. I mean, I know that was his girl, but he could have played it off and at least acknowledged me. I just wanted to pull him to the side and holler at him. After what I'd done, I needed his acknowledgment. I *needed* it. Then, Adina could have her man.

"She's nobody," he told Adina, as he pulled her attention back to him.

Nobody? I felt like shit.

"Get away from my man," Adina shot at me.

Before I could get a word out, DeMarco was in my face with his arms stretched out, protecting her.

It was an eerie feeling.

"Gon', shawty. Don't piss off my, lady."

"Your lady? DeMarco…"

He jumped in my face so suddenly that a few people gasped, assuming that he was about to hit me. "I told you I had a girl," he said slowly through gritted teeth, low enough for only me to hear.

Fuck his girl. "You didn't say that shit a few..."

He cut me off, jumping into my face with so much anger that I got scared. I knew that he was just trying to cut me off to keep me from telling. "Get the fuck out my face, bitch!"

I was so taken aback that I didn't have a comeback. Laughter caught my attention. Adina was snickering. Cordell and the girl that he was dancing with were laughing at me. Hell, even a few other people who heard the confrontation were doing the same. I was mortified. I could still feel his penetration; Cordell's scent lingered on me, too.

I walked away. I made an about face and scurried away in embarrassment, only to bump smack dab into Joi's goofy ass.

"Simone, you okay?"

"Get the fuck out of my way!" I didn't even look back as I pushed my way by her. I kept my head low as I stormed out of the frat house.

79

Chapter Five

Cecily

"You *whaaaaaaaaaat*?!"

I was grinning as Saundra squealed.

"Yes!" Saundra continued to shriek. "About time, gawd damn it! You finally gave him some! Whew! How was it girl?"

As I turned over the bacon that I was frying, I told Saundra about my night with Maurice. Instantly, a Chester cheese smile spread across my face as I recalled the night. It was incredible. For years, Derek had slammed his dick into me with no love; his powerful strokes were full of lust and no emotion. It was good, no doubt. So good that I had committed my pussy to him for nearly twenty years without me asking his permission. However, when Maurice slid his dick into me a few hours ago, it was magical. I was singing like Mariah Carey. He wasn't as big as Derek, but there was a curve in his dick that hit my g-spot with every stroke.

I told Saundra that Maurice was so happy to finally be inside of me that I didn't have to do any work. I lay across his California King in his condo on Michigan Avenue in an orgasmic heaven. He spoiled me with his dick and mouth just as much as he had been spoiling me emotionally and financially. My legs were on his shoulders as he leaned in, kissing me ever so romantically while his dick swam inside of a pussy that was overflowing. I was unsure whether it felt so good because it was good or new...or both.

"Damn," Saundra said with a deep sigh when I was done. "I'm so jealous."

"Don't be. Live vicariously through my vagina until you find a man," I teased as I turned off the burners on the stove.

"I guess I'll have to. At least one of us is finally getting some."

Saundra was just as single as I was. Well, I guess, as single as I used to be. Now that I had slept with Maurice, I was officially his woman.

"Is this my pussy?" he asked as he was delivering to me yet another orgasm at three in the morning. "Please tell me that it's mine. Tell me you're my woman, baby."

Though I was on the brink of an orgasm as I moaned, "Yes, baby. It's yours. I'm yours," I knew that in his heart, I had just officially made a commitment to him.

He hardly wanted to part ways with me that morning. I enjoyed his time and attention. But honestly, I couldn't get Derek off of my mind. He still hadn't returned my calls. It was sad how, even though Maurice had completely rocked my world, I still rolled over and called Derek as Maurice took a shower.

He still didn't answer.

I actually felt like I had just cheated on Derek. My heart and body were so committed to that man.

"My food is done. Let me eat breakfast, girl. I'll see you at work later."

"You hungry after workin' all night, huh?" Saundra giggled.

I had to giggle too. Indeed I had enjoyed a good workout.

"Bye, girl." I was still giggling as I hung up.

Then I went to wake up Simone. I had peeked in on her that morning when I crept in at seven. She was fast asleep. I figured she was at that frat party all night. I was looking forward to having breakfast with her. She could tell me about her frat party, and I could tell her about my date, minus the sex part. Me and Simone had grown so close over the years. After the abortion, I just wanted her to know that she had a friend, as well as a mom.

"Simone?" I knocked lightly and awaited her reply. But when I heard tears, I invited myself in. "Simone, you okay?"

She never said a word. I entered the bed, noticing her balled up in the fetal position.

"Simone...Simone, baby, what's wrong?" I sat next to her on the bed without getting a response. I was prepared to coach her through another heartbreak, convinced that DeMarco had showed his ass at that party.

Little did I know, that was the least of it.

The longer it took her to respond, the more I began to panic. My heart began to beat outside of my chest. Memories of the dramatic ordeal that she got herself into a few years ago made the possibilities of her tears endless.

"Simone, sit up, baby."

Her hair was all over her head. It looked like she still had on the shirt that she wore to the party. I noticed bruises and cuts on her legs and started to freak out. "Simone, what happened?!"

Finally, she lifted her head. My heart dropped, noticing that her lip was busted.

"What happened?! Who did this to you?!"

Her mouth would open and close, but nothing would come out. She looked sick to her stomach. She looked terrified.

"You can tell me, baby." Obviously, somebody had attacked her. "What happened at the party?"

She was barely opening her mouth, but I could make out the words that she finally said. "They took advantage of me."

My blood pressure shot up. The room felt like it was spinning. "Somebody took advantage of you?"

I nodded my head and said, "yes," but apparently my mother took what I said the wrong way.

When I said that, I had no idea the world of bullshit that would follow afterward.

My mom freaked.

"Oh my God!" She began to cry, which made me cry harder. She was looking at the bruises and cuts all over my legs and arms.

"Ouch," I flinched as she touched my arm.

"They hit you?!" She didn't even give me a chance to reply before she was saying, "Let's go. You have to go to the doctor."

She shot out of the room so fast that I didn't get a chance to get a word in edgewise.

I thought that she wanted to take me to the ER to get my bruises checked out. However, I had no idea the extent that my mother was going until I got to the University of Chicago. Everything had gotten out of hand, just as quickly as I told the lie. As soon as we walked into the emergency room, two detectives ushered me into the back.

The doctors and nurses knew my mother, so they took extra special care of me. Nurses and doctors flooded the hospital room. They took pictures of my wounds. They performed a pelvic exam. I panicked, realizing that they were treating me like a rape victim. Yet, having someone there to comfort me, made me feel better. It felt like...maybe...I wasn't as dumb as I felt the night before.

"Can you tell me what happened, Simone? Take your time." The doctors and nurses had disappeared. The female detective was sitting next to my bed, holding a notepad. There was a male detective behind her. My mother was standing in the corner of the room. So much concern was in her eyes. I feared that this would drive her to drink again. Even my father had arrived. He was standing next to her, with his arm around her.

Everyone was just staring at me, waiting on me to say something. I felt so much pressure. I also still felt humiliated. I lay there, replaying the night in my mind. Every time I envisioned Adina, DeMarco, and Cordell looking at me like I was beneath them, it enraged me. I could hear everybody's laughter. I felt sick to my stomach...like it was still happening... like they were still laughing. Truth be told; I did feel violated. I felt completely used and taken advantage of. They played me. They embarrassed me...especially DeMarco!

"They raped me."

I heard my mother gasp for air, and then her tears filled the room.

"Who raped you, Simone?" The detective watched me, waiting for an answer. Again, everyone's eyes were on me.

As soon as I mumbled, "DeMarco Johnson and Cordell Carter," the male detective's eyes bulged.

"DeMarco Johnson?" my father asked surprisingly. "Star basketball player, DeMarco Johnson?"

The female detective shot daggers at my father. "Mr. Campbell, please. Let us handle the questioning."

But my father ignored her. He even left my mother's side and started to walk towards me. "Hold up. DeMarco Johnson, Simone? Are you sure?"

I felt so offended. What the fuck did he mean 'was I sure?' Was that supposed to mean that somebody like DeMarco wouldn't want anything to do with me?

I squealed, "Yes, I'm sure!" with so much confidence. He was looking at me like I wasn't good enough to be with DeMarco, just like that bitch Adina had scorned me. Tears flew from my eyes.

Then he asked me, "Are you telling the truth?"

My mother gasped. "Derek!"

Immediately, the female detective gave him another warning. "Mr. Campbell!"

The male detective made his way towards my father. He grabbed him by the elbow and began to pull him towards the door. "Mr. Campbell, please leave. Now."

He didn't have to force my father out. He glared at me for a few seconds before leaving willingly. My mother watched him longingly as he walked by her without even a goodbye. She looked torn between running after him and staying with me.

She chose me, although regretfully.

She stood close to my bed and held my hand. She even rubbed my forehead as the female detective told me, "I'm sorry about that, Simone. Now, tell us what happened."

I was still hesitant. But as they stared at me...waiting and urging me on...I felt compelled to validate what happened that night to myself.

As I parted my lips and began to tell them my version of the story, the humiliation started to fade away.

Derek

I was happy to get the fuck up out of there. I didn't want any parts of what the fuck was about to happen in that hospital room.

DeMarco Johnson was the hood's Golden Child. He'd grown up in Houston's third ward in the projects. He played street ball and made a name for himself. But he never took basketball seriously until he moved to Chicago to live with his grandmother after his mother died from a drug overdose down in Houston. Soon recruiters caught wind of his skills and offered him a full ride to UIC. His grades were horrible. He never took school very seriously back in Houston. But his skills were so tight that coaches on the team paid every tutor they could to help DeMarco maintain the necessary GPA in order to keep his scholarship. It only took two years for the NBA to start knocking at his door. He was still hood, though. He never wanted the fame; he never wanted to be some fancy NBA player. For years, he denied everyone. Eventually, he gave in to pressure and was now deciding which team to sign with. We all hoped that he would go with the Bulls.

Simone was my daughter. I didn't know DeMarco personally at all. But something didn't seem right. I didn't see DeMarco risking a multi-million dollar contract on getting a piece of pussy. I knew my daughter. She would have fucked a nigga like him willingly, without him even asking. I'm not saying that Simone was a hoe, but she had been caught in questionable situations with guys since she was a teenager. Hell, she was fast in kindergarten.

I just didn't believe her. Something wasn't right.

"Everything okay?"

I nodded in response to Nicky. I had just met her a few weeks prior, so she wasn't due any further details than a head nod.

As I turned the engine of my black on black BMW, I eyed Nicky's dark-skinned, long, thick legs. Her skin was so smooth. Reminded me of dark chocolate. I planned to eat her as such as soon as I got some food in her stomach.

Like I said, I was making up for lost time.

Nicky and I were already on our way to lunch when I got the call from Cecily that I needed to come to the hospital ASAP. At first I didn't trust it. Over the past nineteen years, Cecily had successfully tricked me into her presence with one false alarm after another. But I had really hurt Simone by not being there for her when her mom made her get that abortion a few years ago. So I took a chance that day. Little did I know, Simone was most likely pulling a false alarm of her own.

Chapter Six

Simone

By Monday, things had gotten completely out of hand.

"You hoe!"

"Slut ass bitch!"

"Don't nobody wanna take that stank ass pussy!"

"Bitch, you wish he wanted you!"

I was literally running out of the Student Hall. Various cheerleaders were running after me, insulting me. Adina was one of them.

They already hated me. Ivory Mason, captain of the cheerleading team, went through her boyfriend's phone a few months ago and found out that I was in his dorm room, sucking his dick while she went home to her grandmother's funeral.

Now, this only made their hate for me that much worse.

"We are going to beat your ass!" I heard Adina yelling in that squeaky ass annoying voice.

Thankfully, I made it to my car. I hopped in, trying to catch my breath. My hands were shaking as I tried to turn the engine of my Toyota Camry.

"I can't believe this shit," I breathed.

I was able to pull off just as Adina and a friend made it to my car and started to bang on the driver's side window.

Tears streamed down my face as I drove wildly down the street. I peered into the rearview mirror to see cheerleaders in the middle of the street, still screaming and throwing rocks and debris at my car. I jumped at the sounds of various objects hitting my car.

Luckily, I turned the corner, and they didn't.

When I told the police what happened, I thought that would be the end of it. I figured that I wouldn't look like a liar to my mother and that DeMarco and Cordell would get in a little trouble. I thought the detectives would question them, scaring the shit out of them and showing them that I was not to be fucked with. However, I assumed that once they denied attacking me that would be it.

It didn't happen like that, though. Apparently, by Sunday evening, detectives were hauling DeMarco and Cordell out of their dorm room in handcuffs. The shit had even made the news Monday morning. I shitted bricks as I got ready for school. But since sex crimes victims' names were kept confidential, I assumed it was okay to go to school. Apparently, I was wrong. The news hadn't given my name, but DeMarco and Cordell were furious. They were able to post bail by noon. They told the entire basketball team, which in turn informed the cheerleading team.

I knew that by the end of the day, the entire campus would know.

"*Fuck.*"

"You are not going back to that school."

I rolled my eyes into the back of my head as I sat next to Simone on her bed. She was lying across the bed, crying her eyes out. I was rubbing her back soothingly.

"She can't drop out of school, Cecily," I said.

Cecily was sitting across from us in a purple La-Z-Boy that had been in Simone's room since she was twelve. When I saw it, back then, I figured it was way too mature for Simone. As always, Cecily gave Simone what she wanted… *times two.*

"She can't go back and get beat up every day because she stood up for herself. She can transfer her credits and go somewhere else."

"Whatever, Cecily." I just shook my head. Arguing with her about Simone was pointless. "Do what you wanna do."

"It will only get worse as the trial goes on."

"Trial?!" Simone's head shot up. Disbelief was all over her face. Tears streamed from her eyes.

"Yes, Simone," Cecily answered. "Unless they plead guilty, there will be a trial. You can't keep going to that school with all of this going on. I am sure that DeMarco and Cordell will get kicked out, but those girls won't. They will bully you every day."

Simone just dropped her head down on the pillow and continued to cry.

I didn't even argue with Cecily. I just gave Cecily the same disappointed look that I always gave her. Simone was naive as hell, but she had it honest. Her mother never listened. She thought she deserved and was owed everything. She did what the fuck she wanted to do, despite anybody's feelings.

Like once Simone fell asleep, Cecily did what she wanted to do despite my feelings.

"Stop, Cecily," I was trying to be quiet, not to wake Simone. I was at the front door, trying to get the fuck out of there. Cecily wasn't letting me leave.

"Derek, I've missed you."

She was literally crooning. For once, she wasn't drunk. Well, maybe she *was*—drunk with lust. That's how she had been over the years—intoxicated with lust. Sometimes I wondered if Cecily loved me as much as she claimed, or if she was obsessed with "winning."

"I have to go," I managed to get out as she cuffed my dick. I was wearing some Coogi jeans, but I could still feel her caress against my dick. It hardened against my will. It remembered every time it was inside of any of Cecily's orifices. Her pussy and head were just as insane as she acted sometimes.

"You know you miss me, baby," she whispered as she backed me into a corner. "Don't act like that."

This is how I knew how obsessed this woman was. She should have been worried about her daughter. She should have been trying to figure out a way to make the niggas pay that she believed "raped" Simone. She was more interested in my dick, though.

Always had been.

Just as it always had in regards to Cecily, my dick always conquered my common sense. Common sense told me that this wasn't a good idea. Common sense told me that now that I was single, once I stuck my dick in her, her antics would only get more outrageous. She would only get clingier.

But did my dick listen to common sense?

Did any man's dick ever listen to common sense?

Hell no.

I didn't fight her as she dropped to her knees. I leaned my head back against the wall, asking myself what the fuck I was doing asking for this kind of drama. She had been on me more than usual since Angela died, and it was definitely for a reason.

I felt her wet mouth wrapped around my dick and forgot all about that shit, though.

Cecily

It was so hard to stay quiet. Yes, I had just had some good dick a few days prior. Nothing compared to Derek though. His sex was legendary. His dick was like a museum piece.

"Shit," I breathed into the wall, trying my best not to allow my sex sounds to echo through the house.

My nightgown was gathered around my waist. Estee Lauder foundation mixed into the paint on the wall of the foyer. My face was pressed against the wall. I was arched on my tip-toes. Derek was behind me, giving me some of the best dick I'd had since the last time I had the dick.

He just didn't know what he did to me.

No matter who I dated. No matter who I fucked. No matter how much money I made. No matter how many degrees I had. I was only complete, and I was only whole, when his dick was in me.

The shit was sad; I know!

I knew that he thought the same as well. I knew that he pitied me for panting after him for nearly twenty years. He also was mad at himself for falling for it time and time again.

"Gawd damn…Shit," I hissed.

He was mad at me. He was mad at this pussy. He was mad at himself for fucking me again. He was punishing me with every stroke. His dick was bitch slapping my g-spot with every thrust. He was only making my infatuation for him worse. With every orgasm, I was convinced that my love for him was legit.

Who wouldn't want to be with him? What woman wouldn't want to suck his dick every chance she got?

"Arrrgh!" Derek tried to muffle his orgasm. He was more unsuccessful than I was.

I giggled. "Sssh!"

"Mmmph," he muttered.

I smiled into the wall. He was cumming. That was fine. In fifteen minutes, I had come at least four times. The pain in my toes as I stood on them didn't matter. Each orgasm was award winning. I hated that such an incredible dick was cumming before I could enjoy it giving me an orgasm again. But I was happy that I was the one that was making him feel as good as he sounded.

He huffed, puffed, and cursed until I could feel his babies bursting inside of me.

It was okay. After Simone had turned ten, I was intent on never having anymore children. I was pumped full of Depo-Provera every three months. However, after she was taken advantage of by Twon, I convinced my gynecologist to tie my tubes.

I just couldn't bear being responsible for another life that was bound to be victimized by the assholes in this world.

"You should stay the night." I watched longingly as Derek pulled his jeans up over an ass that was so nice and plump for a man. Clearly, with his build, he'd missed his calling to play in the NFL.

I licked my lips and stared into those intense brown eyes. I'd never seen facial hair that I wanted to rub my fingers through so much.

"I...I can't stay, Cecily." I was unsure whether the stutter was from his continued lack of breath or what.

"Why not?" I smiled. "I'm sure you need the company."

He sighed heavily. "Actually, I need to be alone," he told me as he opened the front door. "Tell Simone that I will call her in the morning, okay?"

I didn't push him. I was happy to have him inside of me again, so I decided not to fight his exit as he vanished.

"Whew!" I was on cloud nine as I floated back into the house. The lustful smile was still painted across my face as I turned lights out all over the house. On my way to my bedroom, I grabbed my cell phone from the coffee table.

"Shit." I'd missed quite a few calls from Maurice. I called him back right away. Not that I felt any guilt or anything. I had briefly told him about what happened to Simone, before Derek got to the house. So I knew that he was worried about both me and Simone.

"Hey, baby."

"Hey you. Sorry about that. I was tending to Simone." Crawling into my bed was such a relief. Those powerful orgasms exhausted me. My body relaxed into the mattress like it formed to my body. I only wished that another body was there alongside mine: Derek's.

"How is she?"

"Not good at all," I said with a sigh.

Maurice sighed as well. "It's only going to get worse if this goes to trial."

"That's what I told her. Hopefully, they'll just go ahead and plead out, though. Then Simone can put all of this behind her. I hate that she has to go through all of this. I am so worried about her."

"Me too. I'm worried about her mama too. You want some company? I don't want my baby to be alone tonight."

I should have been happy. That should have made me smile. However, hearing those words come from his lips made me so sad. The words were beautiful, but to my heart they were coming from the wrong man.

Chapter Seven

Simone

I hated the way that I had to leave school, but I was more than happy to take a break from classes and the drama. Constantly looking over my shoulder was a headache. There was always a chick that had beef with me back then. DeMarco and Cordell getting arrested had only made that worse. My mother was right; I had to transfer.

Until that was done, I was doing nothing in my mother's house day after day. One day, to make the time go by, I called a friend. His name was Aaron Ward. We were neighbors and went to the same grammar and high school. He'd always had a crush on me. I never liked him because he wasn't a challenge.

Typical, right?

He was a regular guy who wanted to take me to the movies and to the mall. That shit was wack and boring to me. There was no intensity or drama.

I wasn't feeling him. But when I was bored, I used him for a good time.

"Man, you hear about DeMarco Johnson getting arrested? That shit crazy." Aaron was stuffing his face with pizza. We were around the corner at Giordano's, getting a bite to eat until I went over to my cousin Jasmine's place to get my hair done. Aaron was so busy stuffing his face with sausage and pepperoni pizza that he didn't notice my eyes roll into the back of my head. I even put my fork down. His mention of DeMarco's name made me suddenly lose my appetite.

"Yea, I did," I mumbled as I glanced out of the window.

"I can't believe that shit. Rape? Really, my nigga? His life is over."

"What do you mean by that?"

"*Shiiid*, a rape charge is a wrap for his basketball career. I bet those teams are tearing up those negotiations left and right." He chuckled like it was funny while I was forcing my vomit to stay down.

"Even if he isn't going to jail?"

"Who said he wasn't going to jail?"

I simply shrugged my shoulders. He barely noticed the color leaving my skin.

"Maybe...*juuust* maybe he won't be found guilty. But even still, the damage is done. I heard that he already got kicked out of school. It's a wrap for that nigga. Game over."

I wanted to reach over the table and put my hands around his throat to shut him the fuck up. I didn't want to hear that shit. DeMarco had been sending me text messages and leaving me voicemails begging me to tell the truth. What I thought was interesting was how he was now blowing up my phone when the son of a bitch was completely ignoring me before.

Fuck him.

It might not have happened like I said it did, but he *did* take advantage of me. I felt violated standing in front of him and his woman looking at me like I wasn't worth the time of day.

Bet he'd think twice about using the next chick.

"Bet you don't have to rape the ladies. You get it thrown at you left and right, huh?" I was changing the subject, but it was true. Aaron was a cutie pie. Light-skinned, nice build, and 5'11". We were the same age. He wasn't in college, though. His father had hooked him up with a job at the CTA right out of high school. He was already driving buses for the CTA and making good money for a twenty-year-old. He drove a tricked out Caddy. His jewelry was so icy. He stayed clean with a fresh lining that surrounded long plaits. He rocked the latest, hottest labels.

He was good potential. In my right mind, I would have just been with him.

That was too much like right, though.

"The one I want ain't throwing it at me, though." He held the most attractive smile on his face as he spoke to me.

I blushed, genuinely. "C'mon now."

"Why is that? I've been chasing after you for years. You turn me down every time."

"How do you know you want to fuck with me, Aaron?"

I just wanted to hear it.

"You're pretty. You're smart...I bet them long legs would look good on my shoulders."

I giggled and threw a used napkin at him.

"Nah, for real," he said as he caught it. "It's not just about sex. I like you. I'm single. You're single. Why not?"

Funny thing is as he sat there telling me everything that a girl would want to hear, I was mad that it was him telling me that. Why couldn't Twon choose me like that? Why couldn't DeMarco fall head over heels for me like that? There Aaron was, wrapped in a handsome, boyfriend bow, but I didn't want him.

Silly me.

I was giggling like a little girl.

"Stop it, Kendrick. Simone is going to be here in a minute. I have to get ready."

He wouldn't listen. He continued to rain down kisses on my cheeks. I couldn't help but giggle. Kendrick was my baby.

"I can't help it," he groaned with his lips on my cheek. "I love my, baby."

"I love you, too...Now get up."

He grumbled as he rolled over on his back, freeing me. As I hopped up, Kendrick smacked me on my bare ass.

"Put some clothes on before I take that shit." With the way that he was looking at me, I was more than willing to let him get this pussy one more time.

But I couldn't.

"I can't, baby." I even poked my lip out. I was so sad to tell him 'no' as I looked at that hard, marvelous dick swaying back and forth as he lay on his back. "I have to do Simone's hair. She's on her way."

Again he grumbled. I left the bedroom. Had I watched him any longer, I would have been on top of his thick, long dick riding him to the point that I almost woke my five-year-old from his nap.

As I turned on the shower, I had such a pleased smile on my face. I absolutely loved Kendrick Smith. We were like soul mates. Being with him felt like hanging out with my best friend every day, until we started fucking. The sex was amazing. Our chemistry in the bedroom was damn near frightening. The dick was what had brought me back twice after I found out that he was cheating. In my right mind, I shouldn't have. I suffered from a lot of trust issues because of it. But, Kendrick meant so much to me that I weighed the pros and cons. It was better having him in my life than out of it. Our relationship was worth more than some slut he fell up in on some bullshit.

I couldn't wait until the day that he changed my name from Jasmine Mays to Jasmine Smith. We had been together for three years. Like I said, we were besties. We did everything together. We clubbed and hit the streets like homies. Then we had the emotional connection of kindred spirits. More than loving me, he understood and rocked with me. When most men only saw my big booty and small waist as a conquest, he treasured my personality and fell in love with it. He was even a father to my son, Marcus. That was a blessing because Marcus' father was killed in a drive-by while I was six months pregnant.

The doorbell rang just as I was stepping out of the shower. "Kendrick, baby, can you get the door? That must be Simone."

I groaned in frustration as I shut off the shower and stepped out of the tub. I had been at work all day. I preferred to spend this evening under my man, not doing Simone's hair. But, duty called.

I did hair on the side while I worked full-time at a research firm. I called homes for eight hours asking parents if their children were immunized. I got hung up on ninety percent of the time because people thought that I was a telemarketer. I should have been a gawd damn stripper. I had the body, and it would have been a lot easier. But I didn't have the balls. So, I slaved at work and did hair in the evenings. All of this in addition to going to school full-time. I wanted so badly to be a teacher. However, trying to live on my own and take care of Marcus was becoming more important than school, unfortunately. It was rough keeping my 1992 Impala running and the lights on in my two-bedroom apartment on 79th and Princeton. Kendrick helped me a lot, but I did more hustling than studying.

As I dried off in the bathroom, I could hear Kendrick letting Simone in as he introduced himself. They'd never met. Simone was my second-cousin. Our mothers were first-cousins. Their mothers—me and Simone's grandmothers—were sisters. We weren't raised together. Every now and then, at a family function, we would catch up. Sometimes she would call, and we would talk for hours. I would tell her about my hectic life—juggling being a single mother to a five-year-old, going to school, and working. She would tell me about her hectic life, but it was hectic for different reasons. I was juggling the responsibility while she was juggling men. She had so many stories of one man after another sweeping her off of her feet and practically begging to marry her. Just recently, she was telling me about some athlete on campus that wanted to marry her. Of course, she hadn't fucked him yet. Simone was always stingy with her pussy. I hadn't really heard from her since. That is, until a few weeks ago when she suddenly wanted me to come to a party with her. I wasn't a college party type chick though. I didn't have the privilege of living on campus. My mother said that I should have gone. Our mothers wanted us to be as close as they were. Obviously Simone was trying since, after the party invite, she now wanted me to do her hair.

"Hey, Simone."

She smiled as I approached her. I smiled as I reached her and hugged her. She hadn't changed a bit since I saw her a few years ago. She was still that perfect tan color. Her features were so sharp and defined. Her breasts were huge, but she could have used a lot more ass.

"What's up, girl? What's been going on with you?"

Before Simone could answer, Kendrick came back into the living room with his keys in his hand. "I'm gon', babe."

I hated to see him leave. He was like my shadow. But he knew the rules. There had been past bullshit from flirty females. So when I did hair in the house, he wasn't allowed to be over. The only reason that I had let him be here this long was because Simone was my cousin.

"I'll be back later," he told me. "I'm going home to shit, shower, and shave."

Simone giggled. I cringed with embarrassment.

"I'll be back. Come walk me out."

I excused myself and followed Kendrick out of the door.

Once outside in the hallway, he grabbed me by the hand. He brought me close to him and kissed me softly.

"Be good," I told him.

"You be good."

"I'm doing hair."

"I don't know. You and your cousin might have some plans. She got a look about her."

I folded my arms and eyed him suspiciously. "What does that mean?"

He just laughed sarcastically. I immediately smacked his arm. "Don't play with me, Kendrick."

"Are you serious? That's your cousin. I would never."

"Oh, only because she's my cousin?"

"I wouldn't do it period."

I rolled my eyes and stepped away. He immediately brought me back towards him.

I tried to fight him. "Stop, Ken."

But he kissed my cheeks. Those big juicy lips melted into my skin. "Stop it, baby. I love you. Don't act like that. I know I've done wrong, but I'm done with that. Trust me."

Derek

"I don't want to be here that long, Nicky."

It was after midnight. Nicky and I had been bar hopping for hours. I was drunker than I wanted to be. I was dealing with Angela's death by keeping myself busy. I was dealing with the rejection of who I really wanted to be with by spending my time with insignificant bitches.

I was keeping myself busy with the wrong things: pussy and liquor.

One of those pussies that I regretted was Cecily's. She hadn't stopped blowing me up since I gave in a few days ago. I regretted doing it the moment I felt her juices run down my dick. There was no way that I should have done that, knowing how she felt about me. I wasn't prepared to give that woman what she wanted. I definitely shouldn't have done it, knowing who my emotions were wrapped up in.

Cecily wanted my heart and, once again, my heart was somewhere else.

"Okay, baby. Just let me buy her a birthday drink. Then we can go."

I was tired. Weeks of run-ins with this and that woman, my phone constantly ringing, and hangovers were all weighing on me. I just wanted to go to my big ass house, lay in my big ass bed...*alone*...and go to sleep.

Nicky looked damn good. She was enticing me to spend the night with her with each sway of her hips. She was wearing a tight burgundy tubed top dress that made her ass look juicy. She had on some sexy ass five-inch heels that I would have loved to see on my shoulders. I liked my women thick in all the right places, and Nicky definitely was that. That dark ass skin got my dick hard every time I stared at her face. It was so chocolaty that I fought the urge to just lean over and lick her.

"Ah 'ight. One drink."

I didn't even have the energy for all that though. Nicky had come over to my crib at four in the morning. She was out with this same friend celebrating her birthday last night. She was drunk and wanted some dick. I obliged but, as I did, my mind wasn't in it. It wasn't even in the room.

I didn't want this. I cheated on my wife sometimes, but I enjoyed having the stability of a marriage.

This random shit was getting to me.

As we entered Reese's Lounge, something told me that we shouldn't be going in there. It was a popular bar. It was a party there damn near every day. Everybody hung out there. I was a popular dude. I still had a rep all the way from back in the day when I slung crack and hoes on corners in the Manor. I was an older legend, and legends in the Chi never died. The older kats were still cool with me, and the younger generation looked up to a nigga. I was bound to see someone that I knew, and I didn't feel like being bothered.

As we walked through the door, the bouncer shook up with me and let us in without checking our ID. I followed Nicky's lead, since she knew where her girl was seated.

"Hey, D'."

"D', what's up, nigga?"

Various people spoke as we walked by. I shook up with the fellas and hugged the ladies, all while Nicky led me through the bar holding one hand.

Nicky's friend's party was in the back bar. It was a lot more room back there. I planned to speak cordially to her girl and grab a seat in the nearest corner until Nicky was ready to go. I didn't even want a drink.

"Nicky! Over here!"

Still holding my hand, Nicky led me to a table full of women. I assumed that the woman standing up was the birthday girl since she was dressed the most scantily and was wearing a crown.

Fuck. I fought the urge to react as I eyed all of the women at the table as Nicky and I approached. *Gots to be fucking kidding me.*

Just my motherfucking luck, the birthday girl that Nicky wanted to come celebrate with was standing right next to Patricia.

"Heeeeeeeeey! Happy birthdaaaaaaaaaay!"

"Heeeeey girl!"

Nicky was too geeked, and her girl was too wasted to notice the fucked up look on Patricia's face.

"Well, hi, Derek."

Ooo, her attitude was so gawd damn stank. She was mad. Real mad. Not only was I standing in front of her holding another woman's hand, but she had invited me to be her date at a party she had to attend and I had declined. I had claimed to be busy with Simone.

Immediately, Nicky and her friend looked between me and Patricia curiously. Patricia looked at me like I was crazy while I unsuccessfully tried to play it off.

"What's wrong with you, sissy?" Nicky's friend asked Patricia.

Great. They're sisters.

"Just wondering why my nigga came walking into your party with this bitch."

I didn't even get a word in edgewise. Shit went ham.

"Who are you calling a bitch?!"

"*You* bitch!"

The birthday girl stood between them, trying to stop the catfight. I grabbed hold of Nicky's arm. Patricia looked at me like she wanted to kill me for even protecting Nicky. That made her go harder, knocking her sister down. Now Patricia and Nicky were face to face, threatening each other. They called each other bitch so much that I didn't want to hear the word ever again. At this point, the shit wasn't even about me. I tried to come between them right as Patricia grabbed ahold of Nicky's hair and started pummeling her face. Patricia was from the Manor; she was from the hood. Nicky was raised in the burbs. She went to a private school. Don't think she ever had a fight a day in her life. Poor girl was getting that ass stomped. Patricia had a grip on that bun so tight that I could damn near hear Nicky's roots separating from her scalp. Patricia was so strong that she knocked both me and Nicky around as I tried to separate them.

"Don't touch my sister! Let them fight, shit!" Now the drunk birthday girl was in my face with her finger damn near in my eye.

I backed away. I was too old and too tired for this shit.

Something had to give.

Chapter Eight

Simone

Even though Aaron said that it wasn't about sex, he sure didn't mind getting in this pussy when I offered it to him.

"Mmmm, baby. This pussy is so tight," he moaned as he then let out a low growl.

After hanging out at Giordano's, we had been together almost every day. Each day, he spent it trying to convince me to be his girl. After years of fucking with guys on the low because I was too young to really date, this was the first time that I had gone on real dates: movies, dinner, and parties. It was fun, but I still couldn't make myself fall for him like he had fallen for me. However, he was doing a good job of taking my mind off of the drama that I had lied my way into and couldn't figure a way out of.

On this particular day, I woke up with love on my mind. Not anyone in particular, but the guys that had broken my heart by choosing their whores over me. I don't know what it was about me that was so obsessed with winning a man's heart. You would think that one broken heart would stop me; that I would finally get the picture. It was the total opposite with me, though. It was like when a man told me 'no,' when he gave another woman his attention, it just made me go harder. When I felt like I wasn't good enough, I got obsessed with proving myself wrong.

I was intent on making myself feel good enough that day. So when Aaron called to see what I was doing, I invited him over.

"H...Hey, babe." He was caught off guard when I opened the door in my bra and panties, but he definitely knew what time it was. His smile said so.

"Hey you. Are you going to come in or just stand in the doorway staring at me?"

Not five minutes later, I was on my back in my bed. He was between my legs, gripping my thighs as he held my legs up. His stroke was rhythmic as his head lay back, and his closed eyes were towards the ceiling.

Good thing, because he couldn't see me roll my eyes.

All that shit he'd talked for years about wanting this pussy; I finally give it to him just to find out that he had some child's penis where his grown man's dick should have been.

This is some bullshit.

I probably should have just stopped him. But hell, I was bored. The head game was good enough that I figured I would at least let him cum before I ended my own suffering.

"Yea, baby. Gimme this pussy."

Oh, shut the fuck up! I looked at him like he was crazy, but he still had his gawd damn eyes closed. His mouth was balled up like he was really doing something. He was sweating like he was really in that pussy laying some serious pipe.

He couldn't be serious.

This was just my luck! For years, I'd been getting completely dicked down by niggas who didn't want a thing to do with me. I mean, straight getting slayed by niggas who wasn't shit. I finally get with a nice guy that wants to date me, and he has a dick the size of a clitoris!

I was even more frustrated then, than I was before he got there. Once again, I felt like a fail.

"You like this shit?"

Really?! I seriously had to hold back a laugh.

The silence was awkward. He gripped my legs tighter, and he started to pound harder; that only made his pelvis bang into me because he was so damn little.

"Aw!"

123

"Tell me you like it baby."

"I like it, damn!"

He didn't even open his damn eyes. I wanted mine to shed tears. I wanted to cry right there, but this fool would only think that I was crying because it was so good.

I could not believe this shit. I needed to get my ass back into school fast. I only found myself with Aaron because I was bored any damn way. I was losing my mind in that damn house. It had been about two weeks, so the news was no longer covering the case. The streets, however, were still talking by way of social media. Back then, we didn't have Facebook. It was BlackPlanet. The message boards were full of gossip, especially those of UIC students. Adina and her cheer buddies were still ready to whoop my ass on sight. Luckily, however, nobody knew where I stayed. The UIC campus was so far west that I would never bump into any of them, as long as I kept a low profile. I was so thankful that DeMarco's family was from Texas. Most of his cousins from down south had threatened to come looking for me on BlackPlanet. The judge had issued a gag order during DeMarco's bond hearing. No one could speak about the case, in particular my name. That was successful ninety percent of the time. When those who knew of the case talked shit online, I was usually "that bitch" or "that hoe."

I felt like a major bitch once Aaron had finally cum. I got out of bed so fast that it made him look at me curiously. "Where are you going?"

"You gotta go," I lied. "My mom will be home soon."

He watched me longingly. He looked like he had a lot to say. Because of that, I avoided his eyes altogether. He had that dick all of his life. He had to know the wackness between his legs. I wasn't bitch enough to tell him, but I wasn't going to lay up with him like shit was sweet.

Thankfully, my phone rang as I slipped back on my shirt. "Hello?"

"Hey, Simone." It was Jasmine. "What are you doing?"

Not a damn thing.

"Nothing, girl. What's up?"

"Wanna go to the mall?"

I was relieved to have an excuse to get Aaron out of my face even faster. "Sure. I'm down."

"Cool. On my way."

It was cool to see Simone that day that I did her hair. We hadn't hung out like that since we were little. Since I wanted to go to River Oaks to get an outfit for me and Kendrick's date that night, I asked her to come along.

"Hey, girl." As I spoke to Simone and walked into the house, I was shocked.

Damn, her mama's house was nice. As I walked into their house in Hyde Park, I was in awe. My mama was a single parent of four. She barely had enough money to keep the lights on in our crib on the West Side when I was little. I remembered that Cecily always kept Simone in the cutest clothes when we were little. She stayed in the shop when I was figuring out how to do my own hair because my mama couldn't afford to pay to get my hair done. That's how I learned how to do hair.

"I'll be ready in a minute. C'mon."

I followed Simone in her room, eyeing artwork on the wall along the way.

This is the kinda shit me and my baby are going to have one day.

126

I was always trying to do better. I always wanted nicer things. I never wanted my son to have to want for anything. I wanted to be able to give him anything he wanted. That's why I hustled so hard.

"What you been up to, girl?" I sat on a chair in her room while she stood in front of her closet to get dressed.

"Girl, nothing," she said with an exaggerated sigh. "Aaron just left from over here."

I smiled, knowing that Aaron was the cute neighbor that was trying to holler. She told me about him while I was doing her hair.

"Oh really?"

"Yea, but it was nothing." Then she smacked her lips. "I ain't feeling him. His thirsty ass." I giggled, and she went on. "For real, girl. He is always trying to get some. Like today; he was over here, begging for some pussy. I told that nigga to beat it."

Laughing, I asked, "Why, girl? You said he was cute, he has a good job, and he likes you."

"Yes, he has a good job. But he ain't ballin'. I get ballers, literally. I told you about my boyfriend at school. He's about to be in the NBA."

She had, and I was hating. Not in a bad way. I thought it was great that my cousin was fucking with a nigga that was about to be in the league, but I wished it were me. I loved Kendrick, but living that life sounded real nice.

"What's up with him, anyway? Y'all still into?"

While getting her hair done, Simone had also told me that she had to break up with her guy because he was moving too fast; he wanted to get married and what not.

"Nothing. He's still calling and sweating me."

"Girl, you better marry that man. He's about to be in the NBA. What the hell is wrong with you? You're lucky as hell."

She looked at me from the closet and smiled. "I am, ain't I? I'll take him back. He just needs to slow down a little. He's doing too much too fast—trying to wife me and make me have his babies already."

I looked her upside her head like she was crazy. "And the problem is?"

She sighed dramatically again. "Nothing. They are just getting on my nerves. Between him and Aaron sweating me, I need some air. Damn."

"Relieve that stress by getting that pussy popped by one of these good men sweating you to be with them."

"Nah, ain't nobody getting this pussy."

"Lame." I rolled my eyes. Simone swore that no man deserved her pussy—not even that ballplayer at school. "I'm no hoe, but I ain't gone front; I would have been gave one of them some by now, the way they are treating you so good."

"That's the thing, Jasmine. Treating me good isn't good enough. That's what they are supposed to do. Dinner and proposals ain't enough for me to give this pussy up."

"I guess."

She just laughed. "I'll be back. Let me go brush my teeth real quick."

As she walked out, I just shook my head. She was crazy as hell. Let it had been me. I would have had that NBA dude's babies in 0.2 seconds. Listening to her tell me her stories about campus life, parties, and the guys made me wish that I had listened to my mother and gone away to school. She wanted me to leave my baby with her, go to some HBCU, and get an education. I was too stubborn, though. I refused to leave my baby. So, full-time work was more important than frat parties and homecomings. All I had time for was to go to class. I knew nothing of campus life. I didn't have friends on campus. My best friend, Tasha, and I partied in the hood. We had been best friends since elementary school. But I hadn't heard from her much lately because she was off with her boyfriend in Cali. He was a street nigga, so they stayed in the air traveling.

Just then, Simone's cell phone rang. I let it ring until the voicemail came on the first time. When it started to ring again, I stood to make sure that whoever was calling back to back wasn't her mother or somebody important. I went towards her bed, where I heard the phone ringing from. As I threw the blankets around, I could smell the sex in them. Then, a used condom fell from inside the sheets, semen evidently inside.

This bitch.

Cecily

"So what's going on with the case?"

I sighed as I looked out of the window of Derek's car. He was sitting in the front of the hospital. I'd run out to meet him real quick. He was dropping off some money that he wanted to give Simone. I was happy to have an excuse to see him. We hadn't talked since the night in the hallway. I had called, but each time he didn't answer.

"Nothing yet. There hasn't been a court date since their bond hearing. One is coming up. They are doing a good job of keeping Simone's name out of the media. She's still depressed about having to leave school, though."

Cautiously, he asked, "You really believe her story?"

I shot him a hurtful look, but he still was staring out of the window.

"Yes, I believe her, Derek. Why would she lie?"

He just sighed and continued staring at nothing.

I could tell that he was still in a funky mood. To get his attention, I slowly put my hand on his thigh. I could feel the definition of his thigh, even through his jeans. Though not erect, his dick was against my hand.

He looked down at my hand. He sighed inwardly.

My heart sank, noticing that there was no lust in his eyes.

"What's wrong, Derek?"

He didn't even look at me. His eyes were still staring blankly at anything outside as he said, "Nothing. I just got a lot on my mind."

He wouldn't even look at me. Nearly twenty years, and he didn't even focus on me long enough to give me eye contact.

"Do you ever think about us being together?"

I can't even tell you where that question came from. I regretted it as soon as it left my lips. I dreaded the answer even more as silent seconds crept by so slowly that the wait was gut wrenching.

"Cecily...," was all he said with a frustrated sigh.

"I know that Angela just passed away. I know that it's too soon to even think about being in a relationship. I was just wondering." I sighed as well and began to bite my nails nervously. I too turned my attention out of the window, since he wouldn't even look at me. "I love you, Derek. I always have. I probably always will. You know that I have always wanted you in my life."

Finally, he let go of his hard exterior. "I know, Cecily. I love you too. But..."

"But what, Derek?" My eager response had made him shut right back down, but I couldn't help it. I was so tired of there being a "but."

"But what? Please tell me what it is about me that doesn't make you want to be with me."

"That's it, Cecily. You can't make me."

"Why don't you *want* to? Have I not shown that I'm loyal? That I'm patient? You're obviously attracted to me..."

"Don't bring that up."

"I'm just saying..."

"Don't make it seem like I just fuck you."

"Well..."

"I don't initiate sex with you."

"You don't hesitate to take it, though."

He blew out a breath and ran his fingers over his head. Immediately, I tried a different approach. "Look, Derek. I don't want to stress you, baby." I used the most feminine, soft tone as I ran my hand over his leg. "Let's not fight. You look stressed. I don't want to stress you out further. I just wanted to know when it could be me and you, because I love you so much. I know that we would be so happy."

"You aren't seeing anyone, Cecily?"

His question stung. It was like he was trying to push me off on someone else; some unknown man that he ignorantly assumed that I could ever love as much as I had loved him for literally half of my life. I swallowed the nausea and found the will to fight and prove my worth.

"No, I'm not." As the lie left my lips, I thought of Maurice. I wished that I could love him as much I loved Derek. I wanted so badly to lose this taste of Derek so that I could fully fall for Maurice. But I just could not shake the obsession. To feel complete, to feel like a woman, I needed this seal of approval from Derek so bad.

Derek

She was lying, and I knew it. Cecily thought that I was the dumbest nigga in the world, apparently.

I was so over this game she was playing. I wanted to smack her hand off of my leg, but I knew that I was so much bigger than her that I would break it...considering the anger and irritation that I presently felt.

This was all a game to Cecily. She didn't love me. She didn't want to be with me. It was all ego and pride. The fact that I didn't want her fucked her up. I didn't feed into the presumption that she had that every nigga should want a woman as pretty and smart as her. I was a challenge, and she needed the win in order to get on with life.

I was tired of me and my dick being a pawn in her games. Though I had fallen for it, I was tired of her bullshit and my own.

"Is that right?" was my response to her lie.

"Yea, I mean, I have dated here and there over the years. But no one has compared to the way that I feel about you."

I kept staring out of the window. I didn't need this pressure. If it wasn't Cecily's needy ass, Nicky and Patricia were blowing up my phone.

After the bouncers had torn them apart that night, it was tracks everywhere. They continued to curse each other out until I dragged Nicky out of the bar. She cursed me out for fucking with Patricia. Patricia was blowing up my phone. Though I ignored her calls, I couldn't ignore the hateful messages she left. But at the end of the day, they were both sweating me to see me again. At this point, I knew that it was no longer about me; it was about one wanting to be with me just so she knew that the other wasn't.

I was so sick of women and their games. Cecily, Nicky, and Patricia were sucking me dry. All they wanted was a dick up their ass, but I was so irritated that I couldn't get hard if I wanted to.

Cecily was saying something, but I couldn't even hear what she was saying over my urge to drive the fuck off. "I gotta go, Cecily."

"Derek, I…"

"Cecily, please!" She jumped at the sound of my voice. I think this was the first time that I'd actually looked her in her eyes since she'd gotten in the car. "We'll talk about whatever you're saying later. I gotta go."

I watched her eyes became glassy. She looked so heartbroken and defeated. She looked like she had so much to say. One thing that I can say about Cecily, she had a hell of a lot of fight in her. But I was a much bigger beast than she ever was. "I'll talk to you later," I insisted as she continued to sit. She knew that she wouldn't. She knew that she would call and that I wouldn't answer for days.

"Okay." She sounded pathetic and sad. She sounded defeated. But I knew that losing this battle would only make her want to win the war even more.

She slammed the door on her way out. I closed my eyes and took some deep breaths. These women were doing way too much, trying whatever they could to get me.

All it was doing was making me miss my wife and my marriage even more.

Chapter Nine

Cecily

I was speechless as I eyed the fourteen-karat white gold tennis bracelet.

"Do you like it?" Maurice actually looked nervous as he rested on his elbows in bed next to me, watching me as I stared at each of the fifty diamonds.

"Of course I like it," I breathed. "This is beautiful, Maurice. What did I do to deserve this?"

Not a gawd damn thing. I chastised myself as Maurice reached over and assisted me in putting on the bracelet.

As he told me, "You finally let me love you," my heart sank.

His sultry brown eyes were so loving as they stared at me. They were burning a hole into my heart with the intense heat of his fire and desire. The sunlight shone on his beautiful chest and abs that were so coated with chocolate that I wanted to dip strawberries in him and eat him.

"You've made me a very happy man these past six months, Cecily. This is just my way of showing you that I appreciate you, baby." Then he leaned over and kissed the piece of my exposed thigh that peeked from underneath the blanket. He added tongue, which tickled my skin and sent chills down my spine. "One of the ways," he added with a low, seductive growl.

As I smiled bashfully, I thought about the day before, how I was literally begging Derek to be with me the way that Maurice was. I sat in my office crying for an hour straight. I was mad at myself for not being able to let Derek go. I was ashamed for continuously putting my heart out there for him to so blatantly ignore it. I was embarrassed that though he had shut me out again, I was prepared to do what I had to do to make him see me.

My obsession with Derek was at that point a sickness, and he was the only cure. I only felt whole when he was inside of me. When he was away, I thought of ways to bring him back to me. In my most loving and romantic dreams, this would have been Derek in my bed; Derek would have been naked with an eager, hard dick, looking at me with love and showering me with diamonds. I wondered why I couldn't love Maurice the way that he loved me...the way that I loved Derek.

Maurice deserved it.

I deserved it.

****

"*Whaaaat?*"

I tore the phone away from my ear as I stirred the grits that had begun to boil.

"He bought me a tennis bracelet," I repeated quietly. Though he was taking a shower in the master bathroom, I wanted to be sure that he didn't hear me. I didn't want Simone to hear me either. She was still sleeping in her bedroom a few feet down the hall.

With a pleased sigh, Saundra said, "I'm so happy for you, girl. Maurice is such a good man."

"Yea, he is," I told her.

"And you better act right too."

"What is that supposed to mean?"

"I saw you getting out of Derek's car outside of the Mitchell building yesterday."

I flipped the sausages as I told her, "So. And?"

"Don't let him ruin this for you."

140

I rolled my eyes in the back of my head. "What is that supposed to mean? He was just giving me some money to give to Simone."

"Mm humph."

"Seriously," I lied. "Damn. Oh ye of little faith. Sheesh."

"Okay, okay. I'm just saying. I have to keep you focused."

I hated that she was right. Even as I made breakfast for Maurice, my mind drifted to Derek, wondering was there someone in his home cooking for him.

I know, I know!

I was obsessed.

Simone

On a Wednesday morning, my mother took me to meet with the District Attorney that was prosecuting DeMarco and Cordell. Her name was Stephanie Zappala. She was an older Italian woman in a bad ass pantsuit that looked more expensive than any Gucci bag that my mother had in her closet. Her hair was long, black, and beautiful. But her face was still and stern, like she didn't take any shit.

Sitting in that room felt so real. A lot of legal jargon went over my head as my mother and her friend, Maurice, sat on each side of me.

I was surprised to see Maurice at the house this morning. My mom looked so very happy to have him there. I had heard of him throughout the years. As I eavesdropped on phone calls with her friends, I knew that Maurice had been chasing after my mom for years.

She was too busy chasing my father to allow Maurice to catch her, though.

Hopefully, since he was here during such an important time, that meant that my mother had finally let him catch her. I heard him calling her "baby" a few times, so it was obvious that they were more than friends. I was glad.

I hadn't seen my mother with a man all of my life. It was time for my mother to move on. My father didn't want her.

"The first court date is in three weeks," Stephanie informed us.

"Will she have to testify?" my mom asked.

"The defense will probably want her to during the actual trial, but that won't be for some time. The court date coming up will be to set a trial date, the defense will want to review the evidence that we have, etc. But we are hoping that they will both plead out. That way we can end this as swiftly as possible, and Simone won't have to be put through the torture of testifying."

Both me and my mother let out sighs. That sounded good. At some point, I thought that I would feel guilty for setting DeMarco and Cordell up, but I honestly wanted them to be punished for how they so blatantly used me.

"A plea would be best for us all," Stephanie said as she looked me in the eyes. She saw me thinking and contemplating. "We're drawing up an offer that they can't and shouldn't refuse. We have some pretty damaging evidence, including Terrell Nixon, who will testify to seeing you leave out the room crying. And, Joi Jenkins, who will testify to your emotional state afterwards and say that she saw you bleeding. It's smarter for them to plead, and I am sure that their lawyers are telling them as much… I don't want you to have to testify just as much as you don't. "

"Right," I agreed with a sigh. "Thank you."

"How much time will they get?"

"With a plea? Two years mandatory and probation. They will have to register as sex offenders."

"And if we go to trial?"

"They can face up to ten years."

I should have had a conscience about that. I should have given a fuck about sending them to jail for ten years for something that I had done willing. But things had gotten out of hand so quickly. It was my reputation against theirs. I looked out for them in that room, just for them to play me. Now, I was looking out for me.

Stephanie saw that I was in deep thought. She thought that I was scared and consoled me. "I am going to do everything that I can to make this short and sweet, Simone. I am going to keep you off of that stand. I don't want you to relive that trauma over and over again. I don't want you to have to suffer the defense's badgering because they will try to trip you up and make you look like a liar."

"Who would lie about something like this?" I cringed because my mother sounded disgusted and in disbelief that anyone would lie about being violated in such a way.

Stephanie told her, "It happens, surprisingly. Many women have made false rape allegations."

"What happened to them for lying?" I asked, trying not to sound too interested.

"They go to jail for perjury," said told me. My heart dropped to the pit of my stomach. Then with a deep sigh, she said, "We won't let them make you look like a liar, Simone. I am so sick of these athletes thinking that they can do whatever the hell they wanna do..."

"Amen," my mom cut in.

Stephanie smiled and put her hand on top of mind. "I'm going to make them pay. I am a bulldog in a skirt. They don't want to fuck with me."

The four of us laughed as she stood to leave. "I'll be in touch."

As she twisted the knob and opened the door to the small room, the room suddenly became smaller. For my mother, anyway.

"Hi, Daddy."

My mother shot daggers at me. Shit, it wasn't my fault that my father showed up to support me.

Stephanie looked between Maurice and my father curiously. She played it off and shook my father's hand. "Mr. Campbell?"

"Yes."

"Nice to meet you. I was just leaving."

"Nice to meet you as well. Sorry that I'm late."

"No problem. I'm sure that Simone and Cecily can fill you in." Then she did the professional nod and made her way out of the room.

Once laying his eyes on everyone in the room, my father was visibly taken aback. I stood to greet him to ease the tension.

"Derek..." my mother was so breathless that it was damn near embarrassing. "... I didn't know you were coming. Simone didn't tell me."

"She told me that the meeting was today when we talked this morning. I wasn't coming at first, but the meeting that I was in got canceled." Then he turned his attention to Maurice.

"Hey, man. What's up? I'm Derek."

I wanted to die. You could have knocked me over with a feather right then. I had no breath in my body. I couldn't breathe.

Slowly, Maurice stood to meet Derek's hand that was outstretched, waiting to shake his hand.

I hopped up. "Maurice, this is Derek, Simone's father. Derek, this is Maurice, my... friend."

I could see Maurice holding back a grimace. I could feel his disappointment. Even Simone looked at me like I was crazy as Derek just smiled through tension. He shook Maurice's hand, which appeared to be weak with disappointment.

"Nice to meet you, man," he told Maurice before turning his attention to Simone. "How did everything go?"

I couldn't hear anything after that. I tried my best to avoid Maurice's burning eyes. I tried my best to hold back tears. I felt like a piece of shit. Yes, Maurice cared about me. He was good to me. But I wanted Derek. I even felt like I was disrespecting him in some way by having Maurice in his presence. I just wanted to curl up into a ball and die right there.

Then, to make matters worse, Maurice reached and held my hand. I knew what he was doing. He was testing me and the commitment that I agreed to have with him. And like an asshole, I tried to play it off. I took my hand from him and acted like I was looking for something in my purse.

"Tuh," I heard him grunt.

"You mind if I go, Ma?"

Simone's words caught me off guard and brought me back into the room. "Huh?"

When Derek looked like he was holding back a laugh, my heart sank to the pit of my stomach.

"Do you mind if I go out to eat with Daddy?" she asked. "I know you wanted to go shopping. Can we do that tomorrow?"

I smiled through shame and the urge to burst into tears. I barely had breath as I felt myself shaking while I said, "Sure, baby. No problem."

Simone happily followed her father out of the room. Derek looked even happier to have an excuse to free himself from the tension.

I moved my feet to follow them. Maurice grabbed me by the elbow—stopping me and allowing the door to close us in.

"What the fuck was that?" he barked.

I played dumb. "What was what?"

He breathed inwardly, seemingly to calm himself down. Even at that moment, he was more to me than Derek ever was. He was making an effort—the best he could—not to hurt me.

"I'm your 'friend,' Cecily?" Before I could respond, he cut me off. "This motherfucker broke your heart over and over again, and you diss me for this nigga?"

There was no more niceness. I could see the anger rising from his face like steam. "Maurice..."

"I can't believe you!"

"I...I..." I couldn't even find the words to say. I was so emotionally fucked up. I couldn't even think. I wanted to run after Derek to explain Maurice. I wanted to run away from these judgmental eyes that Maurice was giving me.

"You still love that nigga!"

"No, I don't," I tried to lie as tears began to fall. I was crying because I knew that my truth was hurting Maurice, and it hurt me that I was hurting such a perfect man. I was crying because no matter how perfect he was, I wanted so badly to leave him standing there in order to run after Derek.

"It wasn't a fucking question!" he shouted. "Look at you! Are you crying for me, or are you crying for him?"

I opened and closed my mouth a few times. Nothing would come out.

"All the shit this nigga done to you! He doesn't even want you!"

I finally found my voice. "It's not about that, Maurice. I didn't introduce you as my man because it's not his business yet. We've only been together…"

"That's bullshit, Cecily!!"

Just then, the heavy wood door to the room swung open. My heart beat heavy in anticipation, hoping that it was Derek, hoping that he had left something. Maurice shook his head in disgust as my eyes darted towards the door.

I hid my disappointment when the security guard appeared. "Everything okay in here?"

Though I told him, "Yes…Yes, everything is okay," I was visibly crying and shaking.

He looked at Maurice, saying, "Sir, you need to leave."

Maurice didn't even argue with him. When he began to immediately walk out of the room, I called after him. "Maurice, wait!"

"Man, fuck you."

"You're my ride."

"Run home the way you steady running after that nigga."

I was so hurt that I was stuck. Even the security guard gave me a judgmental look as he allowed Maurice to walk by and then closed the door.

Simone

"Chi Tung cool with you?"

I looked over at my dad and smiled. He was so cool. Way cooler than most dads. He and my mother were so young when they had me; young compared to other people my age, whose parents were in their late fifties and sixties. My father was handsome. Those not related to him would say he was sexy to be in his late thirties. He maintained a young, what we call now, "swag." That day, his hair was sharply lined, along with full facial hair that was black as midnight. He was the bad boy that every hood woman wanted and that every sophisticated woman was curiously drawn to. His scent was so manly that it buckled any woman's knees. He was so cool that his overt affection was shocking, and was what pulled women in even more. I often remember my mother purring over how his eyes sparkled and his jaws clenched whenever he gave women his sexy face.

But beyond that, he was confident. He never fidgeted. His stare was intense. He was a mysterious and quiet man that hardly ever smiled. That only made him even more alluring to women.

However, on that day, as I looked at my daddy, there was something different under his cool, swagged out demeanor.

"What's wrong, Daddy?"

As usual, he put up a front like nothing ever phased him. "Nothing."

I sucked my teeth as I reached over and turned down the Ron Isley that was playing. "Daddy, don't lie."

"My two favorite girls are on my mind."

I smiled. I knew that I was one of those girls. "Two?"

"Angela." I nodded, acknowledging what he meant without forcing him to go through the grueling task of verbalizing how much he missed Angela.

I hadn't spent as much time as I wanted to with my dad when I was growing up. It wasn't his fault. I knew that my mom put him under a lot of pressure when he was around. When I was old enough to get to him by myself, we hung out a lot and had a lot of fun together. I say that to explain that, though I did not grow up in the house with him, I knew my father. I knew how much he loved Angela. Though he did not verbalize his hurt, I saw how much it hurt him to see her suffering when I would visit her sickbed at their home and in the hospital, right before she passed.

I knew what he meant.

He didn't have to tell me.

"Why am I on your mind?"

"What happened to you and this trial?"

I quieted.

"Do you realize what's happening? What this trial means?" He didn't look at me as he whizzed through the streets of the Southwest side of the city. We were going west on 95th Street. I looked at the people outside of my dad's car who were dancing in cars next to us at lights, laughing, and talking with friends as they walked down the street. I was so jealous of their happiness.

I forced back a frustrated sigh and made myself not roll my eyes. "I know what it means."

"Are you sure?"

"Yes. Why, Daddy?"

"I just want to be sure that you know that this is serious. That..." He was choosing his words wisely, and he better had. "...That because of what they did to you, they will have to go to jail for a very long time. People are going to be upset. This is serious. Real serious, Simone. People are going to be mad at you because the courts are going to take away those boys' futures. You understand that?"

We approached a light, and he looked at me. I avoided his eyes and stared straight ahead. I knew what he was getting at. He still didn't believe me. He still thought that I was lying. He was trying to look out for those niggas, when he should have been looking out for me.

"Do you understand, Simone?'

I whipped my head around and looked him dead in the eyes. "I understand. And I'm glad. Because it's exactly what they deserve."

We kept our stare for a few seconds before a horn honked behind us. The light had changed, and he was forced to drive.

He sighed and patted my knee. "Okay, baby. Okay."

Chapter Ten

Simone

"Hey, girl."

I sighed heavily as I said, "Hey, Jas," and put my car in drive. As I pulled away from Jasmine's apartment on 79th and Princeton, she looked at me curiously.

"What's wrong with you?"

There was a lot wrong with me. My response was, "*Girlll*," along with a heavy sigh, because I just didn't know what to say.

I couldn't tell Jasmine about the court date that was approaching that was stressing me out. I really didn't want to testify. I was standing on my story, but to have to go to court and risk seeing DeMarco and Cordell's famiy, who wanted nothing more than to beat the shit out of me, was wigging me out. The rumor mill had quieted. UIC students on social media were onto the next scandal happening at UIC. DeMarco and Cordell's pages were deserted. I was sure that their lawyers had told them to stay off of the internet.

The state's attorney had found pretty damaging evidence on their social media pages of them talking shit about smashing all kinds of girls on campus, so they had all but shut their pages down.

"My mama is getting on my nerves," was what I told her.

Which was the truth. It had been two weeks since that day at the courthouse. Ever since, she had barely been able to drag herself out of bed.

She was pitiful. When she wasn't at work, she was in her bed until she had to tear herself out of it to go back to work. Every time I asked her what was wrong, she would lie and say, "Nothing." But I knew that it had to have something to do with Maurice and my dad. I hadn't seen Maurice since, and it had gotten to the point that my mom was with him almost every day. And I had heard my mother yelling into my dad's voicemail about not picking up her calls.

"And Aaron is getting on *all* my damn nerves."

Jasmine glanced out of her window at nothing in particular as she asked, "Still sweating you, huh?"

"Yes, and getting on my gawd damn nerves."

He was getting on my gawd damn nerves all right. I couldn't stop his ass from calling me. His persistence only irritated me more because it made me mad that I couldn't get the guys that I actually wanted, to be as interested in me. Sure, I could get some pencil dick nigga to blow me up, but DeMarco Johnson treated me like some whore and wouldn't answer my calls.

The shit wasn't fair.

The more I sat in the house, hiding from my bullshit, the more I missed the company of a man—any man.

There is nothing like sitting alone day in and day out to remind you of how single you are. I was looking forward to spending these warm, summer days under a hot nigga. But it was turning out to be one cold-ass summer.

"Can you take me by Kendrick's mom's house before we hit the mall? I need to pick up some money from him."

Urgh. Great. I grimaced on the inside but told her, "Sure."

Just my luck she started to go on and on about Kendrick. How great their relationship was going. How good the sex was that morning. How he had been helping out with the bills. Blah blah motherfucking blah!

"He loves my big booty." The way she was smiling and dazzling, it was like she was having this conversation with herself. I wasn't even in the car with her. "He's always grabbing it and smacking it..." *Urgh. Whatever.* "... Girl, he even..."

"Can you look in the glove compartment and see if you see some lotion?"

I just wanted to shut her the fuck up. Yea, I was hating. I didn't want to hear that shit. We were supposed to be going shopping, not spending our day talking about Kendrick.

I think Jasmine peeped my mood though. She quieted and sat back in her seat as she handed me the lotion.

I hurried and fixed my attitude. Shit, at this point, Jasmine was my only outlet to the world. I couldn't push her away too. "Go ahead. What were you saying?"

But as she continued, I tuned her ass out. That is until we pulled onto the quiet residential block on the Southwest side of the city that Jasmine had directed me too. The block was full of street niggas with no shirts on and bitches with itty bitty shorts. It was a hot day in May. The block was definitely hot as well. The hottest was Kendrick, who stood on his mother's lawn, shirtless in a pair of khaki shorts, watering the grass of his mother's townhome.

When he saw us, as I pulled into the driveway, he smiled.

Gawd damn. Those were the exact sentiments that I had when he opened the door when I got my hair done at Jasmine's place.

"I'll be right back, Simone."

Ken waved at me as Jasmine hopped out. It was a friendly wave, nothing more nothing less. Yet, the longer that I stared at the sweat dripping down his abs, I wished that it was me that was making him sweat.

Hold up. Is that a bulge? I glanced at the impressive protuberance amongst his pelvis and did not fight hard not to stare. Jasmine's back was to me. She didn't see me slobbering over her man. I wanted him to be aware of me, though. Every now and then he would catch my eye, but he kept tearing away from my eyes to put his back on Jasmine.

Just then, I heard Jasmine say. "I'll be right back, babe. I gotta use the restroom."

Hmmmm. If this were a cartoon, devil horns would be rising from my head at this very moment.

"Hey, Kendrick," I called out through the opened window. "Do you know where I can get some scratches fixed? I scratched my car and would like to get them fixed." Before he could answer, I hopped out of the car to show off my long legs in the short tube top casual dress that I was wearing. Sure, I didn't have as much ass as Jasmine, but no phat ass was more appealing than a woman with a willing and ready look on her face.

"You see?" I asked as I bent over and pointed to the scratches that the cheerleaders left with the flying debris.

"Yea, I see what you sayin'." Though he remained standing in the yard, I hoped that more than the scratches in the paint had caught his attention. "I know a guy."

When I turned to face him, and our eyes met, my knees nearly buckled. *Damn, he's fine.* "If I give you my number, can you have him call me?"

He had a charming smirk on his full, sexy lips as he said, "How about I give his info to Jas, and you can just tell him that I sent you?"

Damn it. That didn't work. But I smiled anyway and said, "Okay. Thank you, Kendrick." And when ours eyes met as I climbed into the car, I knew that he knew what my smile meant.

Just as I could hear Jasmine coming back out of the screen door, I rolled the window back up.

This might not be a cold summer after all.

Derek

She was so beautiful when she walked out of the house. I knew right then that I really loved this woman. Any time a woman looks like she is gliding towards you, instead of walking, you're definitely infatuated with her. When I looked at her eyes and smile, I knew that I loved her. I felt relief, and that feeling was like a breath of fresh air. When I realized that I hadn't felt so content since my wife was living, I knew that I was in love with her.

I jumped out of the car in order to beat her to the curb.

She looked like she was just as relieved to see me as I was to see her. She breathed heavily, but it looked more like a sigh of relief. "Hey."

I hadn't seen her since before Angela passed away. Every time I called her to spend time with her—to admittedly sleep with her, but also to just be in her presence—she refused. I sounded so bad when I called her this morning that she finally gave in to me. And I was so happy. I wrapped my arms around her. Without hugging her suggestively, I just held her so tightly.

"I missed you." I hadn't said those words with so much meaning for another woman in nearly sixteen years. My wife was the first woman that I ever loved, and this woman that I now held in my arms was the second.

"I missed you too." Though very faint, I heard her tears. That's when I knew that she loved me too. And her love was real. Not that obsessed shit that Cecily felt. Not that possessive shit that Nicky and Patricia felt. Cecily, Nicky, and Patricia loved me for themselves. They wanted me for their benefit. It was about *them*. It was about their needs and their wants. It was a selfish lust that was so obsessed with me that, no matter what, they wanted me.

This woman loved me. She loved me enough to be without me if she couldn't be with me the right way. She loved me enough to allow me to mourn my wife how I needed to. She was unselfish. Her love was unconditional. And that's how I knew that what I was doing was right.

We were still holding each other. I could still hear her tears, as faint as they were. She was so tiny in my arms that I was bent over, still holding her with my head resting on top of hers.

"Marry me."

When her surprised eyes darted up at me, it surprised me how weak I felt.

163

It scared me too.

"But Derek..."

"I know it's soon. I know she's only been gone for a few months. But I need you, baby. I love you. I'm in love with you."

She was ashamed. She had always been ashamed of sleeping with me while I was married. We were wrong for that, but the difference between her and bitches like Cecily was that she actually felt bad. We didn't want to sleep together because of the deceit behind it all, but it was fate that we bumped into each other that day at the gas station. I had just left Angela's bedside. When she asked me how Angela was doing, because she hadn't seen me or her in years, she broke down. So did I. We exchanged numbers. She called me that night to check on me, and we talked for hours. Angela lay in the hospital bed next to me, out of it because she was full of morphine. Each night, it was the same thing. When I would need air from the hospital, we would meet. Each time I fell for her more and more. She was there for me so unselfishly. She never came on to me— never flirted with me—and that turned me on even more. She prayed for Angela with me, instead of preying on me.

There were a few times that I fell asleep on her couch with her next to me. Eventually, we would spoon. I missed my wife's touch so much that having her in my arms was like therapy. Eventually, I wanted to be inside of her. I seduced her with touch and taste.

She didn't want to be a mistress. She fought it each time. But I needed her. Angela was so sick during those months of our affair. Although I was spiritually married to Angela, I was physically married to this woman in front of me.

"When Angela died, you said that you didn't want to be with me. You said that you didn't want to be a rebound. But it's been months, baby, and I don't care what people think. I care about being with you. I care about waking up and going to sleep with this feeling that I have with you in my arms." She was still quiet, so I continued to convince her. "C'mon, baby. Be with me. Please marry me."

Cecily

I stood at the island in the kitchen. I was eyeing the bottle of Grey Goose with tears running down my face. I had sense enough to know that I shouldn't drink it. I was just so upset, and I wanted this feeling to go away.

I was so hurt. I felt so stupid. It had been two weeks. Neither Maurice nor Derek would talk to me. It was so typical that now I appreciated Maurice more than ever before. I just didn't realize the part that he played in my life until the part was now vacant. For years, he had been so much to me, and my dumb ass had pushed it away for Derek.

But I loved Derek to the point that it hurt...to the point that I wanted so badly to drown the woman inside of me that was obsessed with him in that bottle of vodka.

"Fuck!" I shouted as I swung my arm and swatted the bottle so hard that it flew off of the table and onto the floor. I stepped over the broken pieces and reached for the cordless phone.

I needed to talk before I did something that I would regret.

I listened to her phone ring, praying that she would answer. I was so embarrassed by what I'd done that I hadn't told her. But she was my only friend, and I had to get this shit off of my chest before I found myself drunk and acting out—showing up at either Derek or Maurice's house.

"Hello?"

I was so relieved. "Hey, Saundra. Can you talk?"

"Yea. I just got in the house from work. Girl, the ER was crazy today. There was a pile up on the Bishop Ford. A school bus was involved. It was crying kids every fucking where." She sighed heavily. "Anyway, what's up, girl?"

As soon as I parted my lips, I started to cry.

"What's wrong?!"

I rested my elbows on the island and just sobbed into the phone. I felt so stupid for telling this same sad story about this same nigga over and over again.

I was too embarrassed to start off saying Derek's name, so I told her, "Maurice won't talk to me."

Immediately, she was cautious when she asked, "What happened?" By the sound of her voice, I knew that she knew whatever happened had something to do with Derek.

I told her. As I told her what happened at the courthouse two weeks ago, I was just as ashamed and embarrassed as the day that it happened.

"You did what?!" I cringed. "You introduced to him as your *wheeet*?!"

"My friend," I squealed.

She groaned.

I agreed with her groan. "I know, Saundra."

"Cecily…" was all that she could say.

But she didn't have to say anything else. I knew exactly what the silence meant. I had fucked up with the perfect man. I probably should have said something for me not to appear like the fool that I was, but it was what it was. I was a fool in love. Yes, Maurice was a good man, and I missed him, but he didn't do to me what Derek did to me. With Maurice. I had spent these last few months trying to feel for him what was already burning in my heart for Derek. I knew Derek. I knew all of him: what he was thinking, his dick, his body, what he liked. I knew how his left eye twitched when he was upset, though he showed no emotion in his face. The right set of lashes was fuller than the other. He liked pickles—but only on burgers, not on anything else. He liked his dick sucked with no hands and a

168

lot of spit. If you looked him in the eyes while sucking, he came quick.

I knew *him*.

That type of love couldn't be learned or faked.

Chapter Eleven

Cecily

I hated how well I knew him. I hated that I knew him so well that I could feel his spirit. On a Saturday, I was in my bed looking at the ceiling. I had to be at work in two hours, but I just could not drag myself out of bed. I still hadn't heard from Maurice or Derek. I was over Maurice by this point. But not hearing from Derek was killing me softly.

As I lay there, I had a feeling. We women, we have a feeling... an intuition...about the men we love. I could hear Simone walking around the house, doors opening and closing. I left the bed to explore. In the living room, I saw her brushing her hair before the mirror.

"Where are you going?"

"Out to eat with Daddy."

"He's here?"

"He's outside."

I should have been ashamed at the way that I hurried past Simone, towards the front door. My heart was beating one hundred miles a minute. I was excited, nervous, and scared—all at the same time. I anticipated seeing him, but I was pissed off that he had ignored me for so long. Then, I was nervous about how he would react to me after meeting Maurice.

I ran out onto the porch to see Derek sitting in the driver's side of his BMW. The windows were rolled up. I had run outside so fast that I didn't bother to slip on any clothes. I was wearing a tattered tee shirt that I'd slept in for years and a pair of shorts. I put it on in an attempt to spend the morning cleaning, but I couldn't get the strength to dust, mop, or anything.

"Derek!"

I knocked on the driver's side door. He casually looked at me, like he hadn't been ignoring me for weeks. As he looked at me, I waited for a sign of how he felt...if he felt anything at all. But I saw nothing but happiness, which I knew had nothing to do with me

He was on the phone, and he was happy. I could tell. Angela's death had taken life from his eyes that had been revived since the last time I'd seen him. The light in his eyes and the sincerity in his smile as he talked on the phone caught me off guard. It put a fear in my heart that only God should put there and that only He could take away.

The window began to roll down, and I heard him say, "Let me call you back."

Then he giggled, and his glee sickened me.

Then, as he put his cell phone in the cup holder, I saw a flash of gold on his left ring finger.

I panicked.

He saw the sheer terror in my eyes and tried to ignore it. "Hey, Cecily. Where is Simone?"

I couldn't breathe. I was hyperventilating like an idiot. "Did you...? Are you?" I don't know whether I couldn't get the words out or didn't want to. "Did you get married?!"

When Derek closed his eyes and took a deep breath, which was my answer.

"Derek!" Before I knew it, I was shrieking and smacking my hands on the roof of his car. At that moment, I didn't know my own strength. "How could you?!"

Mind you, I lived in Hyde Park. It was a summer day. White people were jogging up and down the residential street. University of Chicago students were walking up and down the street drinking iced coffees. Others were riding on bikes, skateboards, and rollerblades. And there I was— in flip flops, with my hair all over my head, beating on the top of a BMW like a fucking mad woman.

But I didn't care. I didn't give a fuck. All I cared about was that fucked up pain in my chest that increased with every second that went by that he stayed silent. I couldn't deny the fact that he had, once again, chosen another bitch over me!

"Who is she?!"

"Cecily, you need to calm down." He wouldn't even get out of the car. He couldn't even face me like a man. "Stop embarrassing yourself."

"Fuck that! WHO IS SHE?!"

"I don't owe you shit!"

"The hell you don't!"

Derek looked exhausted. "Cecily, you and I aren't in a relationship! I don't have to tell you a gawd damn thing."

The tears were flowing. "How could you?" I winced.

"How could I do what?!"

"Who is she, Derek?!"

Suddenly, he jumped out of the car. I was so pissed off that I didn't back down. His anger didn't make me cower. "I don't owe you shit!"

"Yes, you do! We were supposed to be togeth..."

"I never said that I would be with you! Not nineteen years ago, not now, not never! You hear what the fuck you wanna hear. *You* said that I owed you something. *You* said that I would be with you one day. Stop worrying about my dick and who I'm with and worry about you and your gawd damn sanity. You need to worry about Simone. Why do you think she gets into the bullshit that she does? She's as a delusional as her gawd damn mama!"

You would have thought that those words would have pierced through this love that I had for Derek and shattered it. But they went through one ear and out the other. "Who is she?"

Derek was done. He threw his hands up and turned to get back into the car, but I grabbed him. "Who is she, Derek?" I cried. "Who is better than me? Who loves you more than I do?"

Derek's mouth opened and closed as his eyes fell on something behind me.

"Hey, Daddy!"

I turned my back to the house and wiped my face free of tears, but there was no use. I would wipe my face, and more tears would replace the ones that I wiped away.

I didn't want my daughter to see me this way. I could hear her coming close, so I made an about-face and darted towards the house in the opposite direction that she was coming in.

"What's wrong?" I could hear Simone asking as she smacked her lips. "Are y'all fighting?"

I took the stairs, two at a time, as I heard Derek tell her, "Everything is fine. Get in the car, baby."

Fuck him.

"Arrrgh!!!" I shrieked as I slammed the door. "Everything is not fine! It's not fine!"

I was losing my mind. This pain was worse than any pain that I'd ever felt. Worse than the first heartbreak that he'd unleashed on me. Worse than any child birthing pain. I wanted nothing more than for it to go away. Whatever it took, I was willing to do it.

Though it would only be temporary, I gave in to the alcoholic fix. I ransacked the pantry, frantically looking for one of the bottles of vodka that I had picked up and successfully managed to put back down on so many occasions over the last three years.

This time, I picked it up and wasn't willing to put it back down until I didn't love him anymore.

Derek

Cecily didn't love me.

She never did.

She thought it was love. She was hurt because for nearly twenty years, she'd tricked her own heart into thinking that she loved me. But it wasn't love; it was an addiction. She was addicted to the pain. Addicted to the drama. Addicted to the cat and mouse game.

She convinced herself that I was hers, so my dick in her pussy was her only validation in life. Those degrees were nothing; they were tissue compared to the significance that she felt that I brought to her life.

I had become her only purpose in life.

That shit was scary.

"Daddy, you okay?"

I had almost forgot that Simone was in the car. We were supposed to be on one of our many lunch dates, but my mind wasn't there. I had completely lost my appetite. That display that Cecily put on had me spooked. She was delusional. She loved what didn't love her. She had trust in what she couldn't see or feel.

No matter what I told her, no matter how many times I told her that I didn't want her, my sane truth couldn't compete with her delusion.

"Just thinking," I told Simone.

"About mama?"

I held my tongue. No matter what, me and Cecily tried not to put Simone in the middle of our situation. "What you mean about your mama?"

"She wants to be with you, daddy. Duh," she laughed.

"It's not funny, Simone," I shot back before I knew it. I quickly softened the blow. "I'm sorry, baby. I just…It's stressful to handle your mama sometimes."

"She just loves you, Daddy."

I bit my lip. She was just as naive and love struck as her mama. We pulled into the parking lot of Red Lobster. I parked in silence, but I stopped her before she hopped out. "Hold up, Simone. I wanna tell you something…"

She looked at me curiously.

"I've never really had a real adult discussion with you about love. I always felt like you were too young. But now, you're old enough to feel real love and get into real relationships. And I just don't want you putting your heart out there for people who aren't asking for it…"

"Daddy, I know…"

"Just listen. If you never listen to anything that I tell you in life, listen to me now. I am a man, so I know first-hand how they think…If you don't have his respect, you will never have his heart. And don't hold onto a man that clearly doesn't want you. The longer you hold on to someone that isn't for you, the longer you ensure you won't receive the person that is for you. And please don't ever think that having a baby will keep a nigga. If he didn't want to commit to you before having a baby, then having his baby won't make him want to either."

I went on and on, trying to give her as much wisdom as I could that would steer her in the opposite direction than Cecily had gone in and never came back.

"I just want you to be smart when it comes to men. I want you to be strong and use your heart wisely," I told her. "Don't give your heart to a man that doesn't want it or doesn't deserve it. No matter how much you might love a man, you can't make him love you back. The only thing worse than a woman who doesn't have the heart to fall in love is one who doesn't have the sense to fall out. If a man loves you, you won't have to do anything to make him be with you—not sweat him, stalk him, fuck him, or have his baby…nothing. If a man truly wants you, there will never be a wall big enough to keep him out. But if he doesn't, there will never be a wall big enough to keep him in."

As Simone just looked at me, smiled, and nodded, I knew that it was going in one ear and out of the other.

She was her mother's child.

Jasmine

"You're trippin', Jasmine."

"I am not trippin'! She keeps calling you for a reason!"

"I just know her from church, bae."

I rolled my eyes in the back of my head as I turned back towards the stove. I grabbed a spoon and began to stir the spaghetti sauce. I had half a mind to take the boiling pot of sauce and fling it on Kendrick. He was sitting at the kitchen table—in front of the laptop applying for jobs—but he should have been behind me kissing my ass.

Some chick from his church was blowing up his phone. He grew up in church. He had been playing drums since he was five. So, for the longest he had been a hired percussionist at various churches. He went in church, played, got paid, and left. He didn't fellowship. That nigga didn't even own a Bible. So when the fuck did he have time to meet this bitch, Brandie, that kept calling his damn phone?

"I swear, Jasmine, it's innocent," Kendrick said, sensing my persistent irritation. "She's helping me find a job."

My face scrunched up as I mouthed, "She's helping me find a job," behind his back.

"C'mon on, baby. Let's not argue. Your birthday is tomorrow. We are supposed to be having a good time."

Yes, my birthday was the next day, but who cares? This Brandie bitch had blew me. I was celebrating my birthday the following weekend with a house party at my mama's house anyway. So I was free to be a bitch that day if I wanted to.

Men are so fucking naive. Kendrick was fine as hell. He was walking chocolate sex, with his sexy lips, tall and thick frame, and impressionable dick, which prints could be seen in any pants he wore. Of course, the bitch wanted to help him find a job! That was her way in!

Duh!

Even if their relationship was innocent in Kendrick's eyes, this Brandie bitch probably had ulterior motives. And unfortunately my man wasn't wise enough to sniff out a bitch with ulterior motives. He was naive and gullible, like many men. He trusted way too easily, not realizing that these bitches play games and do what the fuck they gotta do to get what they want.

Visions of that bitch, Marissa Baldon, posting subliminal messages about my man on Myspace, gave me a sick feeling as I angrily broke the spaghetti noodles in half and dropped them in water.

A year ago, I met Marissa through a group of friends. We all would hang together, and she would come over to get her hair done. While hanging out and getting her hair done, she and Kendrick crossed paths. As time passed, I noticed that Marissa wasn't hanging out anymore, nor was she getting her hair done. I didn't think too much of it because, like I said; we weren't friends. However, I did notice how she was swooning over this nigga on her Myspace page. Every other day, she was posting these lovie dovie messages about this new nigga she met. Imagine my surprise when I went through Kendrick's phone, drunk and in my feelings because he had been acting funny, and I seen text messages between him and what I knew was Marissa's number that clearly indicated that this new man that she had been posting about was the one that was lying in my bed every night.

Hurt was an understatement. Reading those text messages killed me. I had already looked past catching him up with Kamilya, his ex that he was dating before me. But, that fuck up was three months after we got together. He and I were still fresh, and that bitch couldn't let go. They had been high school sweethearts and were together up until a few months before Kendrick and I met.

I gave him that one. It was the usual fuck up that niggas do: dip back on their exes.

But the deceitful shit that he and Marissa did to me hurt me to the core. That took lying and manipulation, which I didn't think my man, *my best friend*, was capable of.

We were broke up for six months, and it was the worst six months of my life. I had never shed so many tears and have never again to this day. Above missing a hard dick and arms around me at night, I missed my best friend...So I took him back.

I still have trust issues, though.

Kisses on my neck brought me out of my trance.

"Stop crying, baby."

I didn't even notice that I was crying. I wiped my face, as I turned down the burners on the stove.

"Look at me." Kendrick turned me around and made me face him. I hated how attractive he was—how big and tall he was, and how much swag he had. It was like, no matter how pissed I was, as soon as I looked in those beautiful eyes, my anger turned to putty in his hands.

"I'm sorry. How long do I have to relive what happened?"

"You're not reliving anything."

"Yes, I am. Every time you question me about some chick, every time you give me a side eye because you don't trust me, every time you question me because you don't believe me, I'm reliving it." I tried to look away. He was right. I was still bitter. But he kissed my neck again...and again. He was trying to make it right anyway he could, but stubbornly tears still fell.

The memories were still that hurtful.

He was right. I was making him relive it because I relived it every time there was sight of it potentially happening again.

Just as I was about to say as much, the doorbell rang.

I was honestly happy to have a reason to terminate this conversation. I sighed and wiped my face as he told me, "I love you, baby. I'll never do that to you again. You gotta trust me if this is going to work."

I took a deep breath, attempting to get myself together. "I know...Let me go in the bathroom and get myself together. Can you get the door for me? That's Simone."

Simone

After I had finished eating with my dad, he dropped me off back at home. As soon as I stepped inside of the house, I smelled the vodka and heard my mother's tears from a mile away. I grabbed my keys and left. I didn't have anywhere to go in particular. The only person that I could call was Jasmine, so I did. She said that she was in the house cooking dinner for her, Kendrick, and Marcus. All I heard was "Kendrick," so I told her that I would be right over.

I made a stop, though, before heading over there.

Kendrick had been on my mind ever since that day I took Jasmine to his mom's house. He was cool and full of swag. Unlike Aaron, who was sweating the shit out of me, Kendrick played my sexuality and flirtation so cool that I was now drawn to him.

I had to have him.

"Awww," Kendrick sang as he let me into Jasmine's apartment. "Are these for me?"

I peered around the bouquet of long-stem roses with a smile. "You wish. They're for me."

"Somebody loves you," he said as he closed the door behind me.

I sucked my teeth and I sat them down on Jasmine's living room table. "He's just trying to get back in my good graces."

"I see. He's definitely trying hard."

I looked around the apartment for Jasmine. He noticed and said, "She's in the bathroom. She'll be out in a minute."

Good.

When he went into the kitchen, I gladly followed his sexy ass. "Mmm. Is that spaghetti?"

"Yea. Jasmine is throwing down a little."

As he sat down in front of a laptop, I asked, "And what are you doing?"

"Looking for a gig."

I hopped up on the kitchen counter. Sure, I could have sat on the table, but I wanted him to get a clear glimpse of my thighs in this skirt as I sat with my legs slightly opened on the counter.

Damn, he was fine. I felt my pussy getting wet just looking at him.

But I tried to have casual conversation with him, in hopes that he would reveal a way that I could get to him. "I thought you were working. What kind of job are you looking for?"

"I am working. My gig is cool. I make decent money, but I'm trying to do something better."

"Like what?"

"Well, I have a degree in Accounting, so anything in finance would be what's up."

Bingo.

"My mom is a Charge Nurse in the ER at the University of Chicago. She has a lot of connections, especially in Human Resources."

He looked up at me eagerly, excited about the possibilities. I was excited about the possibilities of him finally laying eyes on me. When he did, I smiled. It was seductive. My eyes were sending him subliminal messages that I had some connections that I wanted to make with him my damn self. He was a man. He knew what that look meant.

When he licked his lips, I was sure that he did.

I stared intensely in his eyes as I asked, "Do you have a copy of your resume on that laptop?"

"Yea, I do."

"Cool. Email it to me. I'll forward it to my mom as soon as I get home."

"Cool," he smiled. "That's what's up. Thank you."

Again, I smiled. "My pleasure."

As I rattled off my email address, I could hear Jasmine saying, "Ooooo! Who got flowers?!"

As she entered the kitchen, I closed my legs. I noticed Kendrick watching me do so out of the corner of his eye.

"Are those your flowers, Simone?"

I sucked my teeth and rolled my eyes into the back of my head. "Girl, yea. I had lunch with Steve earlier, and he gave them to me. He's still trying to get in good."

Okay, yes, I bought the damn flowers myself on the way over to Jasmine's. Every time we hung out, she was always going on and on about Kendrick this and Kendrick that. I wanted her to see that I had a nigga sweating me too. Steve was the name that I gave her when I would embellish about me and DeMarco's relationship. I couldn't tell her his real name, because I didn't want her to connect the dots between what I was telling her and what was going on in the news about DeMarco.

"Still trying to wife you, I see." Jasmine went straight to the stove to check on her food.

With her back towards me, I glanced at Kendrick as I said, "Yea. But I'm not ready to settle down." Our eyes met briefly, before he looked back into the computer. But I noticed his knees rocking back and forth nervously.

"Something better might come along."

Chapter 12

Saundra

"Whew!" I sighed as I parked in front of Derek's house. The drive to Elk Grove was long from my house on the Southside of Chicago. As I hopped out of my red Mustang and trotted up Derek's circular driveway, the sun beat down on me. It was so hot. It had to be damn near one hundred degrees, and it was only May. It was going to be a long summer. The light-weight silk floral maxi dress that I was wearing was not helping. I was sweating, so it stuck to me and felt as heavy as wool.

Before I could ring the bell, Faye met me at the door. She was beaming. She had that excited and unconditional happy smile that most newlywed brides wore. "Heeey!"

"Well, hey there, *Mrs. Campbell.*" We squealed and hugged each other tight in the doorway of Derek's, and now Faye's, three-thousand square foot home.

"Come on in, girl."

"I don't know if I should," I teased. "Should I take my shoes off first?"

I was being funny, but also very serious. Derek's home was beautiful. We had all been raised in the hood. Despite how much money I made, I preferred to stay in the city and be close to my job. Luxury was limited on the Southside of Chicago. I also stayed rooted in my upbringing. I kicked it at local bars. I still hung out in the Robert Taylor homes that I grew up in until they got tore down. I even still remembered the GD's prayer that I was taught when I thought I was gangbanging in eighth grade.

Point is; Derek's luxurious home was impressive as hell to a city girl like me. I knew it was to Faye as well. After she and Twon divorced, she really never got back on her feet. She was a single mother of four kids, with little help from Twon, who turned into a complete psychopath once they divorced.

I slipped off my sandals anyway, as I followed Faye through the foyer. When we rested on the couch, I was happy to see that she had two glasses of Moet waiting for us.

I grabbed a glass and took a sip as I said, "So, how in the hell did she find out?"

Faye huffed and puffed as she also took a sip of her champagne. She looked so pretty, though all she was wearing was shorts and a tank. It was that happily married glow and hazel eyes that had her looking so beautiful.

"Girl, he went over there to see Simone. She came outside and saw his ring."

"Umph!" I could only shake my head.

"I told him not to wear it around her until he was ready to tell her."

"Fuck that! Why should he have to do all of that because she's delusional? He can wear his ring if he wants to."

"Have you talked to her?"

"No, she won't answer the phone and she called off all week. She is on schedule to work the midnight shift with me tonight. We'll see if she shows up, though. Supposedly she has 'the flu.'"

Faye pretended to pout. "Poor baby."

I cackled. "You ain't shit for that."

Faye rolled her eyes. "She ain't shit for how she's acting."

I 'bout died when Faye called me last Saturday telling me that Cecily had found out that Derek was married. I knew that, despite reality, Cecily was heartbroken. I called her every day, trying to get her to tell me what was wrong. But she never answered and never came to work.

"Is he going to tell her who he married? 'Cause she gon' die when she finds out it's you."

Okay, so I might be a tad bit shady for this, but hey...I can't control Cecily's insane ass delusions about her and Derek. Cecily's relationship with Derek was all in her head. Sure, I blamed him for fucking her delusional ass, but he never ever told that woman that he would be with her. It was always purely sex, for nearly twenty years, when he and Faye fell in unconditional love in a matter of months.

When Faye called me and told me that she bumped into Derek, neither she nor I thought anything of it. We were just genuinely concerned for him since he was literally watching his wife die. Since Faye grew up with him, she called him to check on him. Eventually, she was there for him a lot. He was there for her too, because she had just divorced Twon. They grew feelings for each other. They had sex, which was shady, but Angela was on her deathbed at that point. Faye felt horrible, especially when Angela died. Derek was ready to be in a relationship with Faye a little while after Angela's death, but she refused to be a rebound. I understood, but it was no doubt that Derek loved Faye. I'd seen him with Cecily. The way he looked at Faye was so different. They loved each other. And after all the heartbreak that Faye suffered at the hands of Twon, she deserved to be with a man that loved her.

After months of Faye refusing to be a rebound, Derek showed up at her house and asked to marry her. They got married the next day at the courthouse. It was simple, but truly a fairytale for two broken hearts that had finally found pieces of another heart to help their broken hearts mend.

Of course, I didn't tell Cecily any of this, and I had no plans to. She and Faye hadn't been friends for years. And just because she wanted to live in this delusional relationship with her and Derek didn't mean that the rest of the world had to.

"Have you told, Twon?" I asked with a raised eyebrow.

Shit, Cecily was in her feelings and all, but Twon was slow singing and flower bringing around this motherfucker. He was so hurt that Faye had left him that you would think that he forgot about *alllll* the times he'd ripped Faye's poor heart out of her chest and fed it to every buss down and random bitch in the street, including her best friend's daughter.

Of course, being a man, his ego won't allow him to see that Faye left him because she was tired of his ass! He will swear it's somebody else. Like, how dare she cheat after he's been cheating all of these years.

Faye's eyes rolled into the back of her head so hard that I thought they were going to get stuck back there. "I finally told him. Since Cecily knows, I figured I'd let the cat out of the bag."

"How did he take it?"

"Bad. Not well at all." She chuckled and so did I, totally oblivious to just how bad Twon was really taking it.

Jasmine

♫ I was like, good gracious ass bodacious
Flirtatious, tryin' to show faces
Lookin' for the right time to shoot my steam (you know)
Lookin' for the right time to flash them keys ♫

My birthday party was underway. My mother's basement was full of people; my friends and family, friends of friends, and even some of Kendrick's friends and family. Kendrick had hired his friend DJ Hi-Speed to play the hottest music. The makeshift dance floor was packed with folks grinding in the dimly lit basement. Spades games were underway at various card tables. Hopefully, nobody was outside smoking weed in my mother's backyard, though. She would've come downstairs and shut the whole party down.

Even my best friend Tasha had managed to come into town and surprise me. She and I had spent the entire day decorating and cooking. We had a spread of finger food on a buffet table in the corner.

I was turning twenty-one, so liquor was on deck! Tasha was behind the bar that I rented, along with tables and chairs. She made drinks like the best of 'em, so she was my bartender for the evening.

I was super cute. I went all out and bought twenty inches of Platinum Remy hair. I sewed it in myself, of course. I cut it into a simple layered style with Chinese bangs, which accentuated my slanted eyes. Tasha was really good with makeup, so she hooked me up. I was even wearing fake lashes. I was wearing an Azzure denim sleeveless jumpsuit with peep toe stiletto sandals. The combination made my ass look better than any of the video hoes on BET.

♫ (I said)
It's gettin' hot in here (so hot)
So take off all your clothes
I am gettin' so hot, I wanna take my clothes off ♫

I was definitely getting hot as Kendrick danced closely behind me on the dance floor. His hands were all over me. He was tipsy and so was I. He kept whispering things in my ear like, "You look so beautiful, baby," "I love you so much," and "I can't wait to get in this pussy later."

Over the last week, I had managed to let go of my anger. He'd checked that Brandie chick. She wasn't calling anymore, so I let it go.

"Kendrick, you better stop." I was giggling like a little girl. Kendrick had spun me around. We were now face to face and lips to lips. He was kissing me so deeply.

Suddenly, he bent down slightly. I was in the air before I knew it.

"What are you doing?!" I squealed.

"Kiss me." His eyes were so glassy. He was either acting out because he was drunk or showing off. But I obliged with no problem. I could hear folks standing around us swooning at our display. I could feel my pussy getting wetter and wetter as he sucked my tongue and gripped my ass.

He finally tore his mouth away from mine to say, "I love you," as he put me down.

Grinning, I said, "I love you too. You want another drink?"

"Yea."

"I'll be back." Then I switched towards the bar. I was feeling myself. It was my birthday. I was looking cute. My man was acting right.

It could get no better.

I can't wait to get that nigga home, I thought as I approached the bar.

Since I was the birthday girl, I went directly behind the bar to tell Tasha what I wanted.

"Hey, Tasha."

"Hey, birthday girl. Want another one?"

"Yea. Kendrick does too." As she began to mix our drinks, I asked, "You want a break? You've been working all night. Don't you wanna enjoy the party? I can ask Simone to come over here."

"Yea. Maybe you should," she said, but her tone threw me off. Then I noticed that she was staring in a particular direction. "You better go over there and get your man."

I looked into her direction and saw Kendrick sitting next to Simone on the couch.

Tasha handed me our drinks, looked me directly in the eyes, and said, "Go get your man."

I laughed and said, "Okay." I had told Tasha about me finding that condom in Simone's bed. She knew Simone just as I did. I would share with Tasha what Simone told me. So finding that condom was just as suspicious to her as it was to me. I chalked it up as it being Simone's business though. If she wanted to lie on her pussy, that was on her. But Tasha didn't trust her as far as she could throw her.

"Here, babe." As I approached the two of them, I handed Kendrick his drink and noticed Simone's demeanor. It was weird. She didn't look like she was having fun, and she looked quite uncomfortable; nor did she move to allow me to sit by my man. I motioned for Kendrick to move his arm so that I could sit on his lap. "What's wrong with you, Simone?"

Even her smile was fake as she replied, "Nothing."

I threw on a fake smile and answered, "Nothing."

She looked like she wanted to inquire further. We hadn't been that close over the years, but I guess that, despite my smile, she could see it in my face that something was wrong. Before she could say anything else, Kendrick had grabbed the back of her neck and brought her face close to his. I crossed my legs and shifted my weight away from them as he began to kiss her.

Motherfucker.

Well, this was awkward. But I only had myself to blame. I had read Kendrick all wrong. While at Jasmine's house that previous Saturday, I assumed that his gestures were flirtation. The way that he licked his lips and stared back at me were clear signs to me that he was going. Then once I got home, I checked my emails. I knew that his number would be on his resume, along with his address. Having so much of his contact information had me geeked. When I opened his email, I was beside myself. It read: Call me if you hear anything. It included a smiley face. He'd sent the message while sitting right there in the kitchen with me, so I read it as a subliminal flirtation.

I hadn't hit him up all week. My mother had been completely belligerent since last weekend. Apparently, my father got married, which was news to me. He hadn't even told me while we were at lunch. My mother was heartbroken and had relapsed really bad. She hadn't even gone to work. When she wasn't drunk, she was sick from a hangover.

It was horrible.

Anyway, because of her bullshit, I hadn't had a chance to call Kendrick. So, imagine my happiness when I got to Jasmine's party and he was drunk. I figured this was my opportunity to seduce the man. I just knew he wanted this pussy, and a drunk mind speaks a sober truth. I watched him as he danced with Jasmine on the dance floor. That shit was all a front to get my attention.

Or so I thought.

I watched Jasmine sashay to the bar. She was feeling herself and, true in all, I was being a hater. I was at the party alone. It was irritating the fuck out of me to see Kendrick all in her face when he knew that I was feeling him. I broke my neck to get his attention when she walked away. When he came to sit by me, I happily took the chance.

"Hey you. Having fun?"

"Yea," he smiled. "You?"

"Sort of."

His eyebrows curled curiously. "Sort of? Why sort of?"

"Well, I wanna dance too."

"Then go dance then, sweetheart."

I locked eyes with him as I used my sweetest voice to say, "I wanna dance with you... in more ways than one."

I just knew it was on and popping. Right then, I imagined me and him ditching this party. It excited me imagining his dick in my mouth. It pleased me to no end imagining Jasmine looking for Kendrick and me knowing that he was with me...inside of me.

But when he said, "Shorty, you trippin'," my bubble was burst, but only a little.

I thought he was playing hard to get. I thought he was testing my loyalty to Jasmine. "Kendrick, I want that dick, baby. I won't tell. I know how to play my role."

He laughed! He actually laughed at me! "You wild, shawty. For real. That's your cousin. What's wrong with you?"

Before he or I could say anything else, Jasmine walked up. I prayed that he wouldn't say anything, but I was prepared for it. It wouldn't have been the first time that a bitch was mad at me. It definitely wasn't the first time that a nigga had fronted me off in front of his girl, but it was definitely the first time that a nigga had turned down the pussy.

I didn't like that feeling at all.

After a week, I'd managed to get out of bed and go to work. I was so sluggish. I had been on a binge for a week. Using vodka to numb the pain and to forget that I had ever seen that ring, I called Derek every hour on the hour. But it didn't work.

Derek was still very married, and I was still very heartbroken.

"Cecily…" A knock on the door scared the shit out of me and made my headache ten times worse. "…Stacy called off. We need you to cover in Trauma 1."

I cursed inwardly as I smiled and nodded at Tim, an RN that often worked the night shift in the ER. "Okay. I'll be out there shortly."

Before leaving out, he asked, "Are you okay?"

His question was to be expected. I looked and felt like shit. My hangover was severe. My hands were shaking, and my head was pounding.

"Maybe you shouldn't have come back to work so soon. Are you still sick?"

I had managed to convince the director of the ER that I had the stomach flu all week. They'd even sent "Get Well Soon" flowers to the house.

"I'm fine," I assured Tim. "I'll be out there in a second."

He reluctantly said, "Okay," and left the office.

When the door was secured, I threw my head onto the desk.

"Get yourself together," I told myself. But there was no use. I slowly lifted my head. The room was spinning. I don't know if it was the hangover or anxiety, but I couldn't think or see straight. But I had to work, so I went into my drawer for my purse. I reached inside for the flask that I brought to work, just in case I needed to take the edge off. It's what I did years ago to aid in making it through my shifts when I needed a drink. A little shot here and there helped me get through a twelve hour shift on many occasions.

Then I popped a Norco to make the headache, and hopefully heartache, go away.

Saundra eyed me suspiciously as I walked through the floor. I walked right by her. I didn't have time for one hundred and one questions. She had been blowing my phone up, despite me sending her a message that I had the flu and couldn't talk. It's like she sensed that I was lying.

"What are we eating tonight?"

We?

I cringed as I heard her voice right behind me. She was pushing herself on me. I knew that she was trying to corner me into some deep conversation about what was really wrong with me.

She was my friend. I loved her to death, but I just couldn't bear to allow the words to leave my lips. I needed time.

Lots of time.

Luckily, right at that moment, paramedics charged through the double doors.

"We've got a pit bull attack! Patient is ten years old!"

The entire ER went into panic. The little black girl was so frail. She was crying her eyes out. The dog had attacked her every limb, even her face. Flesh was pouring out of her wounds. You could even see straight to the bone in some.

"Jesus," I heard Saundra whisper behind me.

We stood outside of the room, allowing doctors to assess her until there was room for us to go. As we stood there for fifteen minutes, I could feel the shots I'd gulped down finally taking effect. The mixture of the Norco and alcohol had me suddenly feeling great. I was on cloud nine and couldn't control the way my eyes rolled into the back of my head and rested closed because I was so relaxed.

"Cecily, you okay?"

I looked at Saundra and rolled my eyes. "I'm fine, girl."

Just then, Dr. Parker stepped out, along with fellows that he was teaching, and instructed me and Saundra to assist the fellows inside in closing the wounds that could be treated with stitches.

"I don't feel like this shit," I said to myself. But I didn't even realize that Saundra was in my face.

"Is that liquor on your breath?" Before I could even fix my lips to lie, she said. "Cecily!"

"Would you shut up?!"

I walked away from her and into the room with her on my heels. I could feel her behind me, judging me, but I ignored her. I went into the supply drawers to retrieve the supplies needed to start the stitches. But as I did, I couldn't fake that I didn't feel dizzy. I even dropped a few of the utensils out of my hand. The metal meeting the floor made loud crashing sounds, attracting attention.

Of course, Saundra was right there as I bent down to pick everything up. "You need to leave," she said as she helped me. "You cannot be in here attending to patients when you're drunk."

"I am *not* drunk."

"You need to leave," she said in a louder tone.

She'd caught the fellows' attention. Though they kept talking to the patient and her crying mother, telling them what was about to happen, I knew that Saundra had gotten their attention, and they were probably ear hustling. I stepped closer to her and whispered through gritted teeth. "*I* am *your* supervisor. You don't tell me what the fuck to do."

I didn't faze her one bit. She stepped even closer towards me. She looked like she was disgusted by me. "If you don't want to lose your motherfucking job, I suggest you leave...Now."

Chapter 13

Cecily

I didn't go home.

I went to the bar. It was an after-hours spot called Murphy's that stayed open until six in the morning.

I sat there for three hours, allowing shot after shot to fuel my anger and to give me courage.

I wasn't alone. I drank with people that I would be embarrassed to walk down the street with or introduce to my real friends. We bought each other shots and took them to the head, over and over again until the sun came up.

I stumbled out of the door, and the rising sun burned my eyes. But no matter how drunk I was, that aching feeling in my heart was still there.

"Who is she?" I just didn't know who this random woman was who had managed to take my position again.

I just had to know who she was.

So I drove to Elk Grove. I listened to all of the fucked up, slit your wrist, heartbreak love songs along the way.

Mary J. Blige was on full blast. I sang Anita Baker so loud that my throat hurt.

It was almost six in the morning when I arrived. It was a rainy morning. It was already eighty degrees. The sun made it humid and sticky. Yet, the birds were chirping. I envied their manicured lawn as I pulled up to the house. I envisioned my car being alongside his in the two-car garage. As I walked up to the house, I looked up towards the second floor where I assumed the bedroom was.

My heart filled with rage as I imagined him lying in bed next to his *wife*.

"Open the motherfuckin' door!!"

I was ringing the doorbell, banging on the door, and kicking it with my foot all at the same damn time. I was sure that I was waking up the neighbors in the three-thousand square foot brick homes on either side of Derek's, but I didn't give a fuck. I hoped that I woke them up, because I wanted them and his wife to know how this motherfucker used me.

I was ready for a fight.

"Fuck you, Derek! Open the gawd damn door!"

I was kicking, screaming and crying.

"How dare you?! You think you can just fuck me when you want to?! You think you can play with my feelings, you son of a bitch?! WHO IS SHE?! OPEN THE DOOR?!"

I was possessed. I was ready to claw this nigga's eyes out as soon as he opened that door.

Yet, all fight rushed out of my body when *she* opened the door.

There Faye stood, in a pink silk robe that ended mid-thigh. She was just as beautiful as she was three years ago. Her fake eyes were still piercing in their honey brown color. Hell, she looked better than she did back then.

She looked *happy*.

At another day and time, jealousy of her happiness would possess and enrage me. But at that moment, I had never been so caught off guard in my life. I couldn't even front.

And the way that she looked at me—that smirk—it was so taunting and judgmental.

"I convinced Derek not to call the police on you, but you need to leave, Cecily."

"Have you all been fucking all of this time?"

She rolled her eyes into the back of her head. "Cecily, please. That's none of your business."

"The hell it isn't!"

212

"We aren't and weren't friends. I don't owe you any explanations. Now, get away from *my* house."

I was still standing there with my eyes bulging out of their sockets with a lost look on my face when the door slammed.

"Uh!" I winced and clutched my chest. I tried to gain some sense of composure as I stumbled away from the house. I didn't know what had me delusional—the liquor or the realization.

I can't even remember driving away. I don't remember getting on I-294 S. I don't remember merging onto I-55 and taking it to Lake Shore Drive. The entire drive was a blur. I saw nothing. I felt nothing, but the moisture on my face from my tears and the pain in my chest. I was absolutely unaware of anything until I heard a loud thud. It was so loud that it snapped me back into reality. It was so loud that I screamed in fear. I hit the brakes so hard that I tapped my head on the steering wheel.

"What the fuck was that?"

Now, aware of my surroundings, I saw nothing. I was in the middle of an intersection on a small street in Hyde Park on 53rd Street. Before I knew it, I was hopping out. I wanted to see what that sound was. I wanted to make sure that I hadn't fucked anything up on my car. My crocs slid on the pavement. It was still raining. I hurried around the front of the car, expecting to see a pothole or raccoon... Not a boy. He had to be no more than twenty-five. He was bleeding from the head. He was unconscious.

My nurse instincts were to assess his injuries. I bent down. I hovered over his body. I wanted to check his pulse. But then I realized that he was most likely dead, and I was drunk.

"Shit!" My eyes darted from right to left, up and down the street. It was so early on a Sunday morning that the streets of Hyde Park were vacant. So I ran back to my car.

"Oh my God! Oh my God! Oh my God!" Suddenly, I was sober. I was fully aware of everything. The woozy effects of the alcohol were gone. I was back in my right state of mind, and reality was hitting like a ton of bricks as I put the car in drive.

I carefully but quickly veered around his lifeless body, watching him lie still in the rain in the rearview as I turned the corner.

"...The victim is twenty-five-year-old, DePaul student, Dwight Epps. His mother says that he took the Green Line every day to go to work. This morning, he was on his way to catch the train, as usual, when he was struck at approximately 7 a.m. by a hit and run driver at the intersection of 53rd and Lake Park. The victim is in critical condition. No witnesses have come forward. We are asking that anyone with any information to please contact..."

I turned. I usually didn't watch the news. I didn't want to hear any mention of DeMarco and Cordell's case. I had only stopped because the picture of the victim caught my eye. He was so cute. Apparently someone had hit him and sped off, but a bus driver spotted him and called 9-1-1.

"Probably somebody drunk," I muttered as I turned the television to MTV.

Speaking of drunks, suddenly I wondered where my mother was. She was supposed to be home by eight since her shift ended at seven. I had been up since about six and hadn't heard a sound from her.

She had been so unpredictable lately that I left my bed and my room and went towards her bedroom, wondering if she snuck in the house without me knowing. I just wanted to make sure that she'd made it home okay.

Just as I peeked inside of the bedroom, I heard the front door opening. Her bedroom was empty, so I assumed that it was my mother coming through the door. "Ma?!"

"Hey, hunny."

"Why are you getting home so late?"

"I had to stay at work late."

As the sound of my mother's voice came into the kitchen, I looked up. My shoulders sank in disappointment, and my face frowned up. She looked like shit. I knew she had been drinking. It was evident all over her face.

She saw the look on my face and tried to lie. "It was a long night. There were like three shootings last night." She turned away and was walking out before I could say anything. "I'm going to take a shower."

Didn't nobody have time for my mother and her shit. She was supposed to be a good role model for me. She was supposed to show me how to be a strong woman—not some weak, feeble-minded bitch—so I let her drunk ass be.

She had too much drama going on when I had more than enough of my own. I didn't stay at Jasmine's party long the night before. I was so embarrassed. It's like after that, Kendrick went out of his way to show Jasmine an abundance of affection. Jasmine looked at me funny when I exited stage left so early, when the party was just starting to get lively. So, I grabbed the cordless off its base as I went toward the fridge.

"Hello?"

I chuckled at how bad Jasmine sounded. She sounded like she was *under* the bed. "Damn, girl. Long night?"

"That's an understatement."

She started to go on and on about how the party didn't end until three in the morning. When she started to gush about the presents that Kendrick had for her after the party, my eyes rolled into the back of my head.

"Girl, he had reserved a room at the Sybaris. We were in the jacuzzi all night. There were rose petals everywhere. Then he gave me a *Gucci bag.* I couldn't believe it. I fucked him until three o'clock this morning."

When I barely replied with, "Oh yea?" she peeped how uncomfortable I was with the conversation.

"What's wrong with you?"

I quickly lied, "Nothing."

But she knew better as she said, "Umph," and changed the subject. "What time is it?"

"About eight."

"Shit."

"Want me to call you back?" I was happy to let her go. I was sick of her and Kendrick… Kendrick especially.

"Nah. I gotta get up anyway." I heard her stretching. Then she asked, "What was up with you last night? You were in some kinda mood. Why'd you leave so early?"

"Ummm. That's what I was calling to talk to you about."

She was cautious as she asked, "What's up?"

I hesitated before asking, "Is Kendrick there?"

She paused. I could tell that the mere mention of his name scared her. "No…Why?" As I sighed heavily, she pushed me to let it out. "What's up, Simone? What's wrong?"

I could also hear some anxiety in her voice. I could hear it in her voice that she feared what I was about to say.

I actually felt a bit of guilty. She sounded heartbroken already, and I hadn't even said anything yet. "I don't know how to tell you this… I don't want to hurt you…But I was hella uncomfortable last night because Kendrick was flirting with me…"

"What?!"

"He tried to come on to me. On the couch. He was coming at me like I'd get with him on the low or something."

I was being a hater. Plain and motherfucking simple, I hated the happiness on her face. If I couldn't be happy, I didn't want her to be happy either.

Beyond that, Jasmine was all that I had. I didn't have any other friends. No one at school was talking to me, not even lame ass, Joi Jenkins. I had to say something to Jasmine before Kendrick did. I knew his past as a cheater, and he had been disrespectful enough to cheat with people close to her.

"What did he say?"

What irritated me about her response was, what the fuck did it matter? I'm her cousin. Me saying that her man was flirting and coming on to me should have been enough.

So I added extra sauce on it. "He sat next to me on the couch. He sat real close to me and asked me what I was doing after that party. I was like, 'Nothing. Is there an after party or something?' And he was like, 'Yea. But, me and you are only invited.'" Jasmine gasped as I continued. "I'm so sorry, Jasmine. But I had to tell you. If he was just flirting, I could have let that ride; especially because of the alcohol.

219

But he was super aggressive. Like he just knew that I would fuck him. I mean, we're cousins. What the fuck?"

Just as I assumed, she believed me. "That motherfucker."

I even conjured up some fake tears. "I'm so sorry, Jasmine…"

"Sorry for what, Simone? It's not your fault he's a hoe."

There was so much venom in her voice. I almost felt bad, but fuck that. Kendrick was a hoe. If not with me, with someone else.

"I just feel bad for being the one to have to tell you this. I wasn't even going to say anything. But this morning, I told Steve what happened. He told me that I should go ahead and tell you. He said you deserved to know because you deserve better. And he's right, Jasmine. You deserve much better than him."

Jasmine

My heart was beating a mile a minute.

I was so pissed and hurt all at the same gawd damn time. I couldn't cry. I wasn't even thinking straight. I was barely listening to Simone as I heard her say, "...And he's right, Jasmine. You deserve much better than him." Just then, I heard keys in my front door.

"Let me call you back, Simone."

"Are you okay?"

"No, but he's coming in the door now. Let me holla at him."

Hollering was going to be the least that I planned to do. This son of a bitch had done the unthinkable.

My cousin?

My motherfucking cousin?

First a random bitch. Then a bitch in my circle. Now, my cousin!

This nigga was doing the most.

I was sitting up in bed slipping on a pair of leggings, when his smiling face appeared in the doorway of my bedroom. He was carrying styrofoam carry-out trays.

"You're drunk ass finally got up," he said with a laugh. "I'm glad you're up. I gotta talk to you about something." Then he handed me one of the trays. "Here. Get something in your stomach."

He'd gone to a nearby truck stop and picked us up some food to soak up all the liquor we'd drank the night before.

The night before… damn, it was beautiful. Just thinking of the good time that we had and the love that we made brought tears to my eyes. When he lifted me in the air last night and kissed me on the dance floor—that was genuine love. It was like literally getting swept off of my big ol' size ten feet.

Tears filled my eyes as I could still feel his penetration from just a few hours ago.

I could hear his words clear as day as if his dick was still giving me that sweet, aggressive penetration while he whispered lovingly in my ear, "I love you, baby." He'd told me that over and over again so many times that I believed that we were going to be together forever. Last night, I finally let go. We were finally happy and in a better place. I was able to let go of our nasty, dramatic and hurtful past and just enjoy him.

And now…this.

"Babe, what's wrong?"

I bit my lips in anger. To hear him call me "babe" like he was the loving man that he pretended to be, pissed me the fuck off. It even pissed me off more that—after this nigga had already shown me his true colors twice—my dumb ass went back to him, asking just to be hurt again.

"Babe? Talk to me." My silent tears were scaring him. He sat the food down on the bed and sat beside me.

I got so fucking mad that I flung my food clear across the fucking room!

"What the fuck?!" Kendrick jumped to his feet.

Then I grabbed his and threw it at him!

It was eggs, bacon, gravy, grits, and potatoes all over the gawd damn place.

"What the fuck is wrong with you?!" There was food all over his white tee and blue jean shorts.

"NO! What the fuck is wrong with you?! My cousin, nigga?!"

I charged towards him and smacked fire from his ass.

He took a deep breath. He bit his lip. I was prepared for him to put his hands on me. Not that he had before, but shit, he had never tried to fuck my family before either.

"You need to calm down," he said.

"No, you need to get the fuck out!"

"What did I do?"

"I hate you! Why do you always do this to me? Why am I never enough for you?! Why do you have to hurt me so bad and disrespect me like this? My cousin, Kendrick? Really?"

He tried to act lost. "What the fuck are you talking about?"

"You know gawd damn well what I'm talking about! It's not enough for you that you fuck these random hoes on the street. It's not enough for you that you fuck the bitches that I party with. Now, you gon' try to fuck my cousin too, bitch?!"

He bit his bottom lip. "Watch your motherfuckin' mouth."

"*No*! Watch your motherfuckin' dick, nigga, and stop trying to put your dick in every gawd damn body. You make me sick! You're fucking embarrassing!"

"I ain't even did shit!"

"Of course, you didn't! You always deny some shit until I catch yo' dick right in some pussy. I'm not gon' be that stupid this time. Get the fuck out!"

He looked at me, not only like I was crazy but also like he was disappointed in me.

The nerve.

He sighed heavily and bent down. He began to pick food up off of the floor as he said, "You trippin'. I help you pay the bills in this motherfucka. I ain't goin' nowhere. I haven't done anything."

"So you gon' stand there and deny trying to fuck my cousin?"

His eyes darted towards me. Before he could say anything, I continued. "That's right, you bitch ass nigga. That's what I thought!"

He had a hand full of food that he threw right back on the ground. "What I say? Don't call me a bitch again, Jasmine."

"What did *I* say? Get the fuck out of my house!"

"NO! You trippin'! I didn't do shit..."

"You know what?!" I couldn't stand the sight of him anymore. I picked up my cell phone and dialed out. He wasn't paying any attention to me. He was fuming as he continued to pick up food from the floor. He had to be doing it because he was nervous—not knowing what else to do or say—until he heard me say, "Yes, I need the police at my house right away..."

"Are you fuckin' serious, man?!"

"Ma'am, are you okay?" the operator asked as she could hear Kendrick shouting.

"No, I'm not. I need the police here to escort my *ex*-boyfriend out, please."

As I told the operator my address, he looked so hurt. But I didn't give a fuck.

"I'm out of this motherfucka!" Kendrick snapped.

"Thank you!" I said as my eyes followed him out of my bedroom. I was still holding the phone and could hear the operator talking to me.

"No, thank *you*. You're just as goofy as your motherfuckin' cousin," he shot over his shoulder. "Y'all can have each other."

Cecily

I was trembling as I made my way through the halls of the University of Chicago's ICU unit.

I wanted to see how that boy was doing. All day, I had been so full of guilt and panic. I even traded my car in for a new one before coming to work.

I couldn't believe that I had gotten so wasted that I did something like this. At that moment, I couldn't imagine putting another drink to my lips.

I had possibly killed somebody...because of Derek and Faye.

At the end of the day...after all of this...it just wasn't worth it.

"Hey, Jaton." Luckily, I knew a nurse in the ICU. Her name was Jaton Lazono. We were both students at Florida State University that happened to both be from Chicago and getting our Bachelor's of Science in Nursing at the same time.

"Hey, Cecily. What brings you up here?"

"I heard about that kid getting hit this morning."

Jaton sighed and shook her head. Her long red locs bounced as she did. Ever since we were in college, she had

227

always dyed her hair a beautiful dark red color that reminded me of wine. The color popped and looked so pretty against her olive colored skin.

"Yea. It's so sad. He had... *has* a daughter. He just got married. Poor kid."

I fought not to, but I wanted to break down. I couldn't believe what I had done. I couldn't believe that I had been so stupid. "Yea...," I said, swallowing the lump in my throat. "Yea, it's terrible. How is he?"

"He'll recover but with a lot of physical therapy. His legs are shattered. There was some trauma to his brain. He'll live... Barely, for a while...But he will live."

I sighed with relief. "Well, that's good, at least."

"Hopefully they catch the son of a bitch that hit him. Whoever hit him didn't even have the decency to call an ambulance before they left him to die. Fucking idiot." I cringed. She sounded so mad, like the boy lying there clinging to life was her own flesh and blood. "Luckily, a bus driver drove by, saw him, got out, and called the police."

"Is he conscious? Does he remember anything?"

"He's in and out. We have him under sedation to help fight the pain. He was able to talk to the police a little, but he doesn't remember anything."

"Hopefully he will eventually," I said, hoping to God that never happened.

"We can only hope so that they can arrest the son of a bitch."

With that, I smiled. "Well, it was good to see you. Wish it was under different circumstances."

"Right. Let's hang out soon and catch up. Dinner and drinks? Well...You don't..."

She left the end of the question open, because she knew that I knew exactly what she was referring to. There was no question that I had a bit of an alcohol problem over the years. It wasn't obvious to strangers, but those that really knew me saw how my personal life was suffering because of it.

"No, I don't anymore," I answered. And I was serious. No drink, man, or piece of dick was worth what happened last night. Even though the sight of that ring on Derek's finger still hurt—even though the sight of Faye standing in that doorway still broke my heart—it wasn't worth a life, either mine or a stranger's.

After hugging Jaton and promising to see her soon, I made my way out of the ICU. I decided to walk from the inpatient building back to the Mitchell building, where the Emergency Room was. It was a beautiful night, and I appreciated finally being able to clearly see and feel it and my reality. Sure, I loved Derek, and it hurt that he had, once again, chosen to love someone else over me. But I would have rather lived with that hurt than live the rest of my life dead or in jail over him. I had allowed his effect on me to influence me to make some terrible and foolish mistakes.

One of those mistakes was standing outside of the Mitchell building as I approached it. It's funny how I had never seen him in the light that I was seeing him at that moment. At that moment, Maurice was a sight for sore eyes. Right then, I saw how beautiful he was. I saw how loving he was. I saw how good of a catch he was.

I saw how stupid I was.

When we caught eyes, he immediately turned to walk away.

"Maurice," I called after him and sped up my pace.

I hoped to catch him in the elevators and that I did, by sticking my foot in the doors just before they closed. As they opened, I caught Maurice rolling his eyes in the back of his head.

"Can we talk, please?"

He immediately said, "no," as he pressed the first-floor button over and over again.

"Maurice, please?"

"Hell no. Go talk to Derek. Oh, wait. Is he ignoring you again?" Then he chuckled.

But that chuckle was phony. He was trying to be hard and mean, but that wasn't him.

"I made a mistake, Maurice. I'm sorry."

"You're sorry because he doesn't want you and I'm the next runner up?"

"I'm sorry because I hurt somebody that was good to me. Better than Derek has ever been."

We reached the first floor. The elevator doors opened, and he practically ran out. He shot back over his shoulder, "You should have realized that a long time ago."

As he left out of the elevator, I was on his heels. But he turned around with such an evil look that it shook me. *Now*, I believed his anger. "Do *not* follow me."

I listened. I stepped back and allowed the doors to close. If Derek didn't teach me anything else, it was to not push a man. After twenty years, I finally got that.

But I did want Maurice; then more than I ever had before. My determination to have him back in my life was different than any obsession that I had with Derek. With Derek, I just wanted to win. But with Maurice, I just wanted to love—unconditionally.

Little did I know, it was Derek that would bring Maurice back to me in a way that I would have never imagined.

"Hey, Saundra."

Saundra looked up from her plate of what looked like leftovers from last night's dinner. She only gave me brief eye contact before giving me a fake smile and looking back down into her food. "What's up?"

I left the doorway of the break room and went on in. I hadn't seen or talked to her since she made me leave work the day before. I knew she was mad at me, but I sat down at the table anyway.

"Thank you," I said genuinely while placing my hand on hers. Right then, I realized how stupid and irresponsible that I must have looked—drunk and stumbling like an idiot. Even more, I knew that I looked like a complete idiot the way that I fawned over Derek for all of these years. Though hitting that boy was a terrible accident, had she never made me leave work, this epiphany would have never come over me. I probably would have kept drinking and eventually would have done something way worse.

"For what?" Saundra was so emotionless that it hurt.

"For saving me from losing my job." She had saved me from so much more, but that would forever be between me and God.

Saundra was my friend. My real friend. So she eventually let go of her attitude with a sigh. "I thought you stopped drinking?"

"I did. I mean, I would socially drink, but nothing as bad as I got a few weeks ago after that whole ordeal with Maurice and Derek." At the mere mention of Derek's name, Saundra rolled her eyes. She thought I was doing the usual—obsessing over him. I assured her, "You're a good friend, Saundra. You've been there for me, more than anybody I know. You've been right all along. I found out that Derek got married..."

"What?" Just as I assumed, Saundra was just as surprised as I was.

"Yea. It sent me over the edge. I was just so heartbroken. Felt like I was mourning a death or something... But anyway, I went home last night and had a long talk with God. I also checked myself. I can't lose my job that I've worked for twenty years because of a nigga that has never risked that much for me."

Saundra looked relieved. For the first time in twenty years, I was making an attempt to let Derek go. My heart wasn't completely free of him. There was still quite a bit of residue on it that was still very much in love with him. But finally I realized that it was time to let go of what wasn't holding on to me. I couldn't understand why it took almost taking a life to get me to that understanding. I even found myself asking God why but, like they say, the circumstances that we ask God to change are often the circumstances that he is using to change us.

Chapter 14

Jasmine

I cringed when I looked at the Caller ID. It was Mrs. Smith, Kendrick's mother.

Hoping that nothing was wrong with Kendrick, I answered. I hadn't heard from him since he left the day before, and I was glad.

I was disgusted with that nigga.

"Hello?"

"Hi, Jasmine." She had an attitude. It was clear in her voice.

"Hi, Mrs. Smith. Is everything okay with Kendrick?"

"No..."

"What's wrong?" I asked, sitting straight up in bed.

"Well...I just bailed him out of jail."

"Jail? What happened?"

"Apparently, you called the police on him yesterday."

"Yea, but I told them not to worry about it because he was leaving."

"Well, they were outside of the apartment by the time he walked out..."

I gasped, cutting her off. "How is that possible? I had just called them."

"You know those police sit right in that parking lot of Dunkin' Donuts. Wouldn't have taken them but a second to get to you."

I sighed, regretting what else she had to tell me. For the first time in three years, she was being snappy with me. So I knew that she was blaming me for all of this.

"He got into it with them. They claim he resisted arrest. They arrested him. Amongst other things."

"Amongst other things?"

"He has a few bumps and bruises. You know how the police are."

My heart went out to him. But, shit, he was hurt, and so was I.

"Was it worth it?" Mrs. Smith asked me.

"Was what worth it?"

"This argument you guys had. Was it worth me having to bail my son out of jail and him getting his ass whooped by the cops? Now he has a record, you bitch!"

That hurt. It brought tears to my eyes. Mrs. Smith was like a mother-in-law to me. Kendrick and I weren't married, but what we had in this little apartment felt like a family. And I really felt like I was going through some sort of a messy divorce.

"You didn't have to call the police on him. He has never and wouldn't have put his hands on you. He would have left eventually, if that's what you wanted. You were just being a bitch…"

"I'm sorry, Mrs. Smith, for putting *you* through this, but I had to do what I had to do. I wanted him out, and he wouldn't leave. But I am going to hang up because I don't want to disrespect you."

She was still calling me names when I hung up. I lay back in bed with tears running down my face as I called my bestie.

"Hello?"

"Tasha…" was all that I could get out as the tears started to flow harder.

"What's wrong, Jasmine?"

I told her everything. It felt like I was being punched in the stomach as I relived that moment that Simone called and changed my life. Kendrick cheating was one thing. It hurt, but I could and was getting past it. But to try to do it with my family was something that I couldn't ignore. He had made it so that I could never take him back, even if I wanted to. He had killed our relationship with an unnecessary moment of lust.

When I was done, Tasha didn't reply in the way that I expected her to. "You believe that bitch?"

I was caught off guard. "I…I mean…Why would she lie?"

"Why would she lie about fucking that nigga when you found that condom in her bed? Obviously that bitch likes to lie on her pussy." I was taking it all in as she sighed and said, "I don't know about this, Jasmine. Kendrick has done some foul shit, but your cousin? I don't think he's that low. I told you that I didn't like that bitch. It's something off about her. She looks like she has it all together on the outside. But, on the inside, she is not all there. I can see it."

I groaned as her words began to sink in. She was right. Simone *had* lied to me about fucking Aaron with the same genuine emotions that she had when she was on the phone telling me about my man. "Urgh."

Cecily

I had to take my butt to church and repent.

I felt so guilty for what I had done. I hadn't done it on purpose. I wasn't in my right state of mind. He would live, but the guilt was eating me up.

When I walked through the doors of Holy Spirit, Pastor Harrison was already up giving his sermon. It was a Wednesday night Bible Study service, so not many people were in the sanctuary of the small church. Therefore, when the door creaked as I opened it, many had the natural reaction to turn around. I caught eyes with Saundra, who I knew would be surprised to see me. She'd invited me to church so many times, and I would never show.

However, who I was surprised to see was Faye and Derek sitting comfortably next to her. They turned around to see what Saundra was looking at. When they saw me, there was no emotion on their faces. I meant nothing to them to the point that my presence did not affect them one way or the other. They both gave the Pastor back their attention, once they saw me.

I stood in the aisle dumbfounded, staring at the back of their heads. Finally, the Pastor actually stopped preaching and said, "Come in and have a seat, sistah."

Now that the entire church's attention was on me, I bolted out of there. My heels click-clacked against the hardwood floor as I scurried out of the sanctuary. Beyond being hurt, I was embarrassed. I had been pouring my heart out to Saundra for years. She knew how I felt about Derek. But now she was the third wheel to their love.

"Cecily! Wait! Why are you leaving?" I could hear Saundra calling after me as I ran through the lobby of the church. "Don't leave."

I charged towards her. "Are you serious?!"

Saundra frantically looked around to see if anyone could hear how loud I was. I realized that, yes, I was in a church. So I turned around and stomped outside.

She had the nerve to be right behind me. "C'mon now, Cecily. You came for a reason. Don't let them stop you."

I spun around on my black Prada pumps that I'd excitedly paired with my short sleeve black maxi dress. I was excited about coming to church. I was excited about this new revelation that I was feeling. I was finally getting back to happy—a happiness that had nothing to do with

Derek. And what happens? He still finds a way to creep into my life and fuck it up.

"Don't talk to me like you give a fuck! How long have you known?" Now I was looking at her like *she* was the disappointment.

She didn't try to lie. She sighed and, for once, she was ashamed to tell me something. "For a while."

I waved my hand, dismissing that bullshit. "All these years you've been judging me for loving him! You've been telling me to get over him...that he wasn't any good for me..."

"He wasn't! He isn't!"

"But he's good for her?! You can support them, but you couldn't support us?"

Saundra sighed. "Cecily, there was never anything between you and Derek. Faye and Derek...what they have is..."

My mouth dropped. I couldn't believe this bitch. "What they have?! Are you serious?! You don't see anything wrong with that?"

"No. Cecily, he was not your man. He never was. She doesn't owe you anything. Neither does he."

"He doesn't owe me anything?! Saundra, are you serious? He played with my heart. He knew that I loved him. That I wanted to be with him. And he stuck his dick in me every time I offered."

"C'mon now, Cecily. You know that that man never told you that he would be with you. He never did. That's evident to you, me, and everybody else."

Tears interrupted her. "He hurt me."

"You let him. Hell, you asked him to, if you ask me. You were shown multiple times that he does not love you. Sometimes we wonder how a particular person can hurt us over and over again, causing us so much pain. We have to realize that when God closes a door, he doesn't intend for us to go around back or try a window. *You* did this. *You* caused this hurt."

"Did I cause you to be a fraud? Did I ask you to be a fake friend too?"

She didn't have any deep analogies for that shit. She just stood there, looking like the fake bitch that she was.

"Fuck you, Saundra."

I turned away from her, popping the lock on my truck that was parked a few feet anyway. I didn't hear anything else from her. All I could hear were our heels against the pavement going in different directions.

"Fuck them," I mumbled as I opened my car door. "Hypocrites sitting in church together. They can have each other."

I yanked on the vanity mirror once inside of my car, pulling it down and looking at myself. Looking at myself in that mirror, at my tears and my hurt, I was so ashamed of who and what I saw. Still, I was crying over him. He had married someone else, and I was still hurting over him.

It was crazy how far I'd gone and how far things had gone all in the name of this one man.

They say love will make you do some crazy things.

That is so true.

Faye sighed and ran her fingers through her long, pretty hair.

Damn, I loved her hair. So rare for a black woman to have her own hair.

And I loved her. More than I thought I could ever love a woman. Maybe more than I loved Angela because, after losing Angela, I cherished this wife more and more every day because I knew that she could be taken away from me at any moment with no warning.

"It's going to be okay, baby," I promised her as I kissed the top of her head.

"He's acting like a fucking lunatic. And Cecily is being a drama queen." Again she sighed heavily. "This isn't my idea of the honeymoon stage."

Both of our exes were in their feelings about Faye and me getting married. Cecily was an emotional wreck when Twon was threatening both me and Faye with physical harm. I don't think that nigga ever got over me whooping his ass and popping his ass for knocking up my daughter. I had made him look like a bitch in front of his family. We were older, but there was still a street code embedded in all of us that kept Twon and witnesses from snitching the day that I shot him. But I always got back word through the streets that that nigga hated my guts after that.

But who wouldn't? Then his wife had the nerve to leave him and marry me? He was hot and convinced that she'd left him for me. She hadn't, though. I was just there for her. Just like she had shown me a love that kept me away from people that didn't deserve me, I had shown her the same.

"It's driving me crazy," Faye groaned into my chest.

"Are you giving up on me?"

"Hell no."

"Are you happy?"

She softly ran her nails over my chest. That shit made me feel crazy. My dick was hardening under the blanket as she told me, "I'm so happy."

"Then fuck that nigga."

She lifted her head and peered into my eyes, smiling. "You're such a thug."

I smiled seductively and bit my lips. "You love it."

Before placing her lips on mine, she promised, "I sure do. I will forever."

I pulled my lips away from her and told her, "Promise you'll never leave me."

I meant it. I needed to hear it. I had post-traumatic stress. I enjoyed how much I loved Faye. I enjoyed being married and having a woman there for me when I woke up and when I went to sleep. But every time I felt myself falling deeper and deeper, I was reminded of how you can lose the person you love—just like that—with no explanation from God.

"Promise me, baby."

She cupped my face. Her soft hands against my beard were everything in the world to me. She looked deep into my eyes with those eyes the color of the setting sun and told me, "I'm not going anywhere," as she reconnected our kiss.

Chapter 15

Simone

"Mama, whose car is that in the driveway?"

"Mine." She looked at me and smiled from the island in the kitchen.

"When did you get it?"

"The day before yesterday. Before I went to work. Do you like it?"

"Yea! That's hot, mama!" I was shocked when I looked out of the window a few moments ago and saw a silver 2003 Benz truck sitting in the driveway. "What made you get a new truck?"

She casually shrugged her shoulders as she sipped her coffee. "It was time for an upgrade." Then she gestured towards the stool next to her. "Come here. Sit down."

It was a breath of fresh air to see my mom awake and alert. There wasn't a hint of liquor on her breath. Her hair was combed. It was a complete turnaround from how she'd been moping around the house for the last couple of weeks.

"You look good," I told her as I admired her hair. It looked freshly washed and had so much bounce.

"Thank you. I know I've looked a mess lately." Then it's as if her mind wanted to drift off somewhere, but she shook it off. I knew what she was thinking. I was hurt that my father had gotten married too. I was hurt that he didn't even involve me in the ceremony. Even if it was at the courthouse, I would have liked to be there. I wasn't surprised, though. My mother had told me the same story over and over of how he got married when I was four without telling her. He just showed up with a ring on his finger one day.

"So guess who your father married."

"Who?" I quickly asked.

Her eyes rolled into the back of her head as she answered, "Faye."

"What?!"

She simply nodded.

"I'm sorry, mama."

"Why are you sorry?"

"I mean...I know that you have feelings for daddy."

Her eyebrows curled, and she looked a bit embarrassed. "You do?"

"Yea. It's been pretty obvious all of these years." Then I slightly chuckled to make her feel better and more comfortable.

"Well, then, I'm sorry."

"For what?"

"For not being a better example of a stronger woman. Don't ever wait around for a nigga to choose you. You *make* him choose you up front...You hear me?"

Just that quick, her eyes went from normal to possessed, so I simply said, "Yes, ma'am."

She noticed that she had snapped that quickly, so she attempted to soften her approach. But I still saw the rage in her eyes. "I just don't want you to put yourself in the position to have your heart broken over and over again. It's best that you learn from my mistakes instead of making your own."

"I understand."

"These niggas will chew you up and spit you out if you let them." Then she sighed heavily. "Speaking of which, DeMarco and Cordell's court date is today."

"Humph," was my only reply. At this point, DeMarco and Cordell's legal problems were the furthest things from my mind. I was on to the next, but hey; the damage was done, so I had to continue to roll with it. No matter what, they had definitely played me. They deserved whatever they got.

"You don't have to worry about testifying, though. I talked to the District Attorney this morning. She said that they are pleading out. They will enter their pleas today in court and be sentenced at their next court date. So, this nightmare is over at least."

I sighed with relief, saying, "Good. I'm glad," just as the doorbell rang.

"Get that for me, baby. I have to go get in the shower."

We both left the kitchen, going into different directions. I started wondering what to do with my day. I had no options, really. In just a few months, I had ruined the small circle of female and male friends that I had. Though Jasmine wasn't mad at me, I planned to leave her alone for a few days to allow her to deal with Kendrick.

"Who is it?"

"Is Simone here?"

I peered the peephole and saw an old lady standing on the porch. She had to be damn near eighty years old.

I opened the door, prepared to shoo her away, assuming that she was a Jehovah's Witness or something.

"Hi. May I help you?"

Instead of forcing a Watchtower pamphlet into my face, she shoved her old, crusty finger with its aged dark nail into my face.

"You tell the truth! Tell the truth!" She was so angry that she was shaking.

My eyes bulged out of my head. That's when I noticed another older gentlemen at the bottom of the stairs, but he wasn't as old as she was.

"What are you talking about? Who are you?"

"You go down to that courthouse and tell the truth. DeMarco didn't do what you say he did, and you know it. Don't ruin his life like this. *Please.*" I could see the tears in her eyes. She was pleading and begging. My heart would have gone out to her if I gave a damn, but fuck that.

"DeMarco is an asshole and deserves everything he gets. Now, he'll think about hurting the next woman."

As I slammed the door, she started to shout. "Please?! Tell the truth. You're ruining his life. He's lost everything. Please…" Her voice trailed off in sobs and wails, as I secured the front door. I peered through the peephole to see the man rushing up the stairs to help the old lady. She was so wracked with pain that she was nearly losing balance.

"Mama, c'mon on," I heard the man say.

"No! It's not right what she's doing!"

"We shouldn't be here, mama."

My heart was beating a mile a minute. I wanted them to hurry up and get the fuck away from the door before my mother got out of the shower. I didn't need them implanting the idea into her head that there was any reason to doubt my story.

If I had anybody in this world, if anybody loved and trusted me, it was my mother.

"Should have taught that motherfucker not to be such as asshole," I muttered as I watched the man help the old lady down the steps.

I didn't feel one ounce of sympathy for her old ass. DeMarco and Cordell would hurt for two years behind bars. But for me, it felt like the heartbreak and embarrassment would never go away.

Jasmine

"Damn, they gave them niggas two years," Shawn said as he hung up the phone.

Tasha and I looked at him curiously. Shawn was Tasha's boyfriend. I was chillin' with them at his place. I couldn't be in the house. I was going crazy there. I didn't know what or who to believe. Kendrick wouldn't answer my calls so that we could talk about it. Shit, I wasn't even sure if I wanted to talk about it.

I felt like shit, to say the least.

"Who got two years?" Tasha asked Shawn as she passed him the blunt that she had rolled for him. She didn't smoke weed, but she could pearl a blunt better than anybody I knew.

"My nigga, DeMarco."

Tasha and I just looked at him, lost.

"One of the ball players that got hit with that rape charge at UIC," he explained.

Tasha still didn't know what he was talking about, but I had heard about it on the news.

"Oh," I replied. "That's fucked up."

"Ain't it, man? Lying ass bitch. Wish I knew who the fuck that bitch Simone was. I'd fuck her up my damn self."

I damn near choked while Tasha's eyebrow raised in suspicion. "Hold on. Who?" she asked.

"He told me the whole story. He was fucking with the broad, but she was salty that he had a girl, I guess. She willingly got down with him and Cordell at some party. She was on some freak shit and fucked both of them *willingly*. Cried rape when DeMarco played her afterward." He stood as he said, "Says her name is Simone or some shit like that." Then he told us, "I'll be back. About to smoke this blunt outside real quick."

My eyes were the size of golf balls. As soon as Shawn locked the door behind himself, Tasha and I freaked.

"*Biiiiiiiiitch*," Tasha squealed.

"Omg!" I hopped to my feet, pacing back and forth.

"Didn't Simone say that she had a man that played basketball at school?"

I nodded, trying to wrap my head around all of this. "But she said his name was Steve."

Tasha sucked her teeth as she reached over and grabbed Shawn's laptop. "Bitch was probably lying about that too."

I could hear her pecking on the keys as I replayed so many instances of Simone bragging to me about Steve, even recently. "Maybe she was fucking with two guys on the team. But she never told me about anybody raping her."

"Well, the team roster says that DeMarco's middle name is Steve."

I gasped. "Shut the fuck up!"

"I swear. Look!"

I sat next to her on the couch. There it was clear as day: DeMarco Steve Johnson.

I couldn't even say anything as I recalled the flowers that she brought to my house recently, claiming that he bought them for her.

My fucking cousin was a psychopath.

"Man, that bitch is crazy," Tasha said, revealing my own thoughts.

"Please don't tell, Shawn. I do not want to be put in the middle of knowing this shit." Whether Simone was lying or not, I wanted no part of the shit. Word on the street was that DeMarco and Cordell's friends and family wanted to seriously hurt Simone. I wasn't trying to get hurt in their process of getting to her through me.

"I wouldn't do that to you, friend, but you need to call Kendrick and apologize. If that bitch can lie about a whole relationship—about a rape—she can definitely lie about your man trying to fuck her. Think about it; if she was so uncomfortable, why would she sit there? Why wouldn't she move her seat? I watched the bitch the whole time. She didn't look uncomfortable to me."

"Urgh," I grunted as my head fell into my hands, and a sickening feeling of guilt came over me.

"Yea, friend," I heard Tasha say. "You fucked up...*Bad*."

Cecily

"Maurice, would you please stop and talk to me?"

I was following Maurice around the ER like a puppy.

"Cecily, I'm trying to work, and you should be too."

I grabbed his arm and made him stop. There were only a few nurses and doctors around. The ER was fairly slow. It was only eight in the evening. But I didn't care who saw me. I wanted Maurice to talk to me and to hear me out.

"Please?" I begged. "It will only take a second."

He looked at the x-rays in his hands. He was most likely on his way to one of the examination rooms to explain to a patient the extent of their injuries. But reluctantly, he stopped walking and gave me his attention. We were standing off to the side, near the entrance of the ER, where no one could hear us.

"I'm so sorry, Maurice."

He leaned against the wall behind him as he glanced at nothing down the hall. "Yea. Me too."

I stood in front of him to make him look at me. At that moment, my eyes were much more appreciative of the sight of him than they had ever been before.

He was a blessing.

"You were right. I shouldn't have blown you off like that in front of him. You didn't deserve that, and neither did he. He never put me on the pedestal that I put him on, that you put me on." Again, he was avoiding my eyes. He was being stubborn and hard, but I still saw some love in his eyes for me. So I begged. "I'm over him. It's over. I'm done with that part of my life. Please give me another chance. Give me a chance to love you like you have...."

Suddenly, the Emergency Room doors flew open. Maurice and I had to jump back to avoid the collision. Paramedics were rushing through the doors pushing a gurney and screaming. "We have a gunshot victim! Two gunshots to the back..."

The entire ER staff began to hustle in panic. I followed the team into Trauma 1.

"Sir?! Sir, talk to us!" They were trying to keep the victim alert. If he was alert, that meant that there was some hope that he would live, which was something that we always appreciated in the ER. "What's your name?"

As I rushed to the side of the bed to assist, a gasp full of terror left my throat. I had only felt that much fear a few days prior when I'd accidently hit that boy. The doctors and EMT's looked at me like I was crazy as tears fell from my eyes. "His.... His name is Derek Campbell."

Jasmine

"Get the fuck away from my door, Jasmine!"

"Kendrick, please!" I was crying and begging. I probably looked pathetic to his neighbors that had poked their heads out of their doors and windows to be nosey when they heard the commotion. I didn't care how I looked, though.

I wanted my man back.

"Bye, Jasmine." But he didn't want me back at all.

He was standing in the doorway of his mother's house, holding the screen door open. I was trying to force my way inside, and he would lightly push me back. He even had the nerve to have his shirt off. He was barefoot and in basketball shorts. Just looking at him made me want to just die. I couldn't believe what I had done!

My heart was completely broken, and its pieces were pouring out of my eyes. "I am so sorry, Kendrick."

"I don't want to hear that shit, Jasmine! You called the fucking police on me!"

"I was mad!"

"Because you was listening to another bitch! I kept telling you that you had to trust me."

"I'm sorry!" I was heaving and sobbing. I wanted him back so bad that I was willing to do anything. I just wanted this pain in my heart to go the fuck away. This shit hurt! Like, it literally hurt to know what I had let that damn Simone allow me to believe.

He was trying to close the screen door, and I was holding onto the knob on the other side pulling it back open. I could even hear neighbors snickering, but I didn't care. I fucking loved this man with all of my heart. The chemistry between us was like nothing I thought I would ever feel again with anyone, and to know that I let that evil bitch convince me to turn on him was hurting almost as bad as the thought of losing him. I deserved the anger that was in his eyes as he glared at me.

But I deserved another chance. The chances that I'd given him should have counted for something. The fact that I'd hurt him so bad that he didn't even want to give me that felt like being stabbed in the heart over and over again.

"Kendrick, what was I supposed to think? It's happened before..."

"But what did I tell you, Jasmine? How are we supposed to be together if you don't trust me? If any bitch can come tell you anything about me and you believe it? And now I gotta fight a fucking case? I'm cool on you."

261

When he went to close the door, I freaked. "Kendrick, no! Wait!"

I knew that once that door closed, I would never see or talk to him again. But this time he pulled it with such a hard tug that if I didn't let go, I would break my arm. I let go, reluctantly. He slammed the screen door. Right after, the front door slammed so hard that the house seemed to shake.

I just left. It was over. I saw it in his eyes. I was not dead. But as I walked to my car, I experienced an emotional death. Emotionally, he had just buried me. To see him look at me with so much hate was heartbreaking. He was my best friend, my end all and be all. But that was the last time that I ever saw him. For weeks, he ignored my calls. Eventually, I stopped trying.

For years, I never thought I'd ever find another love that was even remotely close to what Kendrick and I had. And I hadn't until...

Chapter 17

Cecily

Derek clung to life for a few hours, but he eventually died from his injuries.

It didn't feel real. All my life, I had loved one man. All my life, I saw myself with one man. Now, he was dead... and so was Faye. They were gunned down outside of Red Pepper's Lounge. Faye was able to identify Twon as the shooter before she died on the scene. Witnesses say that as Derek and Faye left out of the lounge, celebrating their recent nuptials with friends and family, Twon came out of nowhere firing.

Twon was found in the garage of his home with a self-inflicted gunshot wound to the head the next morning.

"Mmmm." I moaned as I felt Maurice's hand rubbing my shoulders and back intensely as I lay with my back to him, spooning against his warm, strong body.

"You're awake. Can't sleep?" Even though he had just woke up, the evidence of it in his raspy voice, the sound of voice was so comforting that I nestled further under him.

"No. I've been up for a while." I hadn't been able to sleep much for days. Thoughts of Derek kept me up at night. Memories of watching the life leave his body left me afraid to close my eyes, in fear of the possible nightmares.

"Its four o'clock in the morning," Maurice reminded me.

"I know."

Maurice never left my side the night that Derek died in the ER. When they pronounced him dead, Maurice was right there. When I broke the news to Simone, Maurice was right there. When I fought to help her keep her composure, he fought with me. When I broke down as they closed Derek's coffin the day before, Maurice was right there, holding me and telling me how much he loved me.

Again, as I lay there mourning the love of my life, Maurice was right there. He moved my hair out of my face and whispered in my ear, "I love you."

A genuine smile spread across my face as I told him, "I love you too." And I really did. My love for him may never be as strong or intense as what I felt for Derek, but the recent events of my life taught me to appreciate Maurice nonetheless.

As he continued to rub my body soothingly, I rolled over and looked him in the eyes. I could barely see him in his dark bedroom, but I saw *him*; his compassion, his thoughtfulness, his commitment.

When I kissed him, he was surprised. I had been so busy mourning that we hadn't consummated our renewed relationship. I knew that he wanted it, but was respecting what I was going through. In the back of my mind, for the past couple of days, I had wanted nothing more than to pull his body on top of mine, thanking him for all that he had been to me. Unfortunately, between the tears and mourning, the time was never right.

But as I lay in that bed, with his hands on me, with his undeniable love in my heart, I had to have him inside of me.

"Thank you," I told him in between kisses. As I breathed, "Thank you for loving me," tears came to my eyes.

His response was lustfully aggressive. He pulled my naked body on top of his. He grabbed the back of my head as he sucked my tongue. My body shivered in reaction and leaked with excitement. His dick jumped, poking me in my stomach as I lay on top of it. I easily slipped my arm between our bodies, brought it to my pussy and slid down on top of it, all without breaking our deep, passionate kisses.

"Gawd, I missed you," he growled.

I couldn't even respond. The sensation between my legs had me tongue tied. What I felt inside of me – what I felt between Maurice and I – was different and unlike anything that I had ever felt before.

It was then, for the first time in my life, that I made love.

Simone

It was unbelievable that my father was gone.

I felt like it was all my fault. Twon would have never had this hate for my father if it weren't for what Twon and I had done. My father would have never shot him, and maybe my dad and Faye would have never gotten together, if Twon and I would have never had sex.

I also couldn't believe that Twon had done all of this over Faye.

That's when I first learned how deep a man's love can go. If he truly loves you, he doesn't want to share you with anyone and he can't live without you.

It had been a week since they were killed and a day since my dad's funeral, but it still didn't feel real.

"Simone, can you go get the door for me?"

My mother was surprisingly holding up well. Maurice was back by her side. I was glad that he was there for her because she needed that support now more than ever. Every day I expected to wake up to my mother drunk and a mess, but she stayed sober throughout the entire ordeal. That had everything to do with her reconnecting with Maurice.

"May I help you?" It was awkward to see the police at the door. There had been a lot of police presence in our lives since my father's murder. But I didn't recognize the two White detectives standing on our porch as the detectives that were investigating the shooting.

"Is Cecily McMillan here?"

"Yes. One second, please."

I left them on the porch, as I jogged through the house to get my mother out of her room. She had just come home a few hours ago. The smile on her face lit up the house as she strolled in. Now she was standing at her bed packing an overnight bag. She was going back to Maurice's house. Her hair was pulled back into a ponytail, and she wore a simple tee shirt and jean shorts. She looked comfortable and at ease, despite all that she had been through.

"Some detectives are at the door for you."

She looked confused as she said, "Really? Okay."

I followed her towards the front door, wondering what to do with myself that day since I would have the house to myself. I didn't have many options. I hadn't talked to Jasmine since I told her that Kendrick was trying to come on to me. I'd tried to call her with no answer. I expected her to at least reach out to me once my dad was murdered. But I heard nothing, and she didn't even come to the funeral.

"Hi. May I help you?"

I stayed back as my mother talked to the detectives at the door, sitting on the couch to listen. I was totally expecting them to say something in regards to my dad, but they didn't. "Hi, Miss McMillan. We have a couple of questions for you...."

"Regarding?"

"An incident that occurred a few weeks ago, the morning of May 17th. A young man was a victim of a hit and run in this neighborhood. We have been canvassing the neighborhood for trucks that fit the description of what he described..."

"What kind of truck was it?"

"Well, he was only able to remember that it was cream. DMV reports say that you own a cream Range Rover. Is that correct?"

"I did."

"Where were you the morning of May 17th at around seven o'clock?"

"I was home. I was initially at work. I was working the night shift, but I left early. I wasn't feeling well."

My heart started to beat a mile a minute. I

remembered that night crystal clear. That was the night of Jasmine's party. I remembered waking up looking for my mother and her returning home at eight something that morning. I also remembered watching the news and hearing about this same incident that they were talking about.

"Can anybody verify that?"

"Sure. My daughter can."

Damn! Now I was supposed to lie to the police again!

"Was that your daughter that answered the door? Can you tell her to come answer some questions?"

I was so wide-eyed when my mother stepped back and motioned for me to join her at the front door. The way that she stared into my eyes was telling.

I knew what she wanted me to do. As soon as I looked in the eyes of those detectives, I said, "I overheard your conversation. My mother was here all night."

"Are you sure?"

"Yes. I was at a party until around midnight. When I got home, she was here. I got up to cook breakfast at about seven. I couldn't sleep."

"And she was home?"

"Yep."

He nodded and said, "Thank you. That's all then. Sorry for bothering you ladies. Have a great day."

Me and my mother smiled and shook their extended hands. She had no emotion as she closed the door behind them, and she avoided my questioning eyes. But I didn't need her answers. I already knew the truth.

Our bond was unbreakable after that. She had made a mistake. A huge mistake that she will have to live with for the rest of her life. But I couldn't bear to see her in jail because of it. She was now changed, and she never had another drink. I loved my mother so much more that day. She was proof that we make mistakes, but you do what you have to do to look out for yourself. Though I don't think she ever loved another man quite as much as she loved my father, she and Maurice were together for four years. Ultimately she broke up with him when she realized that her heart just could not allow her to love him as much as she loved my father.

I respected my mother so much for that. Her heart was so loyal to who she loved until the day that she died from a heart attack on December 16, 2011.

****

As I lay on that bed, naked and cold, watching Jimmy approach me, with thoughts of my mother in my mind, I refused to go down without a fight. Like my mother, I had made mistakes. Hell, the mistakes that I made were way worse, but I refused to go down like this.

My heart began to beat out of my chest as his hand came closer and closer to my face. However, I was relieved when he ripped the duct tape off my mouth. It burned, and I knew that he had also ripped skin off as well.

But I began to plead through the pain. "Jimmy, please, don't..."

His smile was so evil that I stopped mid-sentence, but he began to taunt me. He stood back and looked at me. "Don't what? Kill you? Like you did Tammy?"

"She was fucking somebody else anyway! More than one person! Fuck that bitch."

He just shook his head and came towards me. Again, anxiety filled my body. He was over me, so close that I could smell his stench. I could feel him untying me.

"Jimmy, please don't kill me. We can go on the run together. Didn't you like this pussy, baby? You felt so good inside of me. I can love you better than Tammy ever did. She didn't love you like a man like you needs to be loved. She deserved to die. I can make it up to you, baby. Just let me."

My hands were now untied as he stood straight up and looked at me. Jimmy's head tilted as he stared at me. There was so much disgust in his eyes. "I think you're more of a monster than I am."

Now, he was untying my feet. "Where are you taking me?" I asked.

He chuckled. "I can't kill you in my apartment. Get dressed."

When he bent down, I could see that my clothes were on the floor beside the bed. He was picking them up to give to me. Now that his attention was on something else, it was like a light bulb went off in my head. I took my chance. I attacked him with all of the strength in my body. I hadn't eaten. I was dehydrated. I was battered and bruised from both his and Omari's beatings. But the adrenaline rush had given me strength that I didn't think that I had.

I kicked, screamed, and bit, all while trying to get the knife out of his hand. If I could only get that knife, I was prepared to cut him from the top of his head to the soles of his feet.

As we wrestled, I finally saw the knife fall to the ground. He was so busy trying to get ahold of me that the knife was no longer his focus. But it was mine. So as he wrapped his arms around my waist, I reached for it, grabbed it, and began to swing, hoping that the flesh that I was slicing would subdue him.

"Arrrgh!" He let me go in order to use his hands to protect himself from the blade, but it was of no use. I was on top of him, attempting to force the knife through every vital organ that I could. "Arrrgh!"

"Die, motherfucka!" I wanted him to die, so that I could live. Yes, I had done some pretty fucked up things. I had taken three lives. But I'd be damned if I was going to go out like this.

Not like this, is all I kept thinking until finally Jimmy stopped moving. Blood was everywhere—on me, flowing from him, and even in my eyes. But I could see my clothes that had gotten scattered everywhere during our fight. I scooped them as fast as I could, while standing over Jimmy as he clutched his chest while it bled out. Then I ran into the living room frantically with the knife still in my hand. I was looking for his car keys, which were thankfully on the couch. I was shaking as I threw my clothes on and frantically looked down the hall towards the room where I left Jimmy. His moans were now faint and became more and more in the distance as I darted out of the house.

The sun felt incredible as it hit my skin. I thought I would never feel the sun ever again. But as I jumped into Jimmy's car and turned the engine, I began to feel the sweet feeling of relief. I quickly drove away from the building. Once I approached a street sign, I realized that I was in Calumet City. I also realized that it was not over. I was out on bail for murder, and I had nowhere to go. I couldn't go to the hospital. I couldn't go back to Omari. I didn't have any money. I had nothing. As I drove, I used a towel that I spotted in the back seat to wipe my face free of blood. It stunk and smelled like gas.

I wished that I could just go somewhere and start over; I wanted a chance to do it all over again. But what was fucked up was that, even as I envisioned starting over, I doubted that if in the same position that I would do anything differently.

I ain't shit; I know.

I was an evil and vindictive bitch, and the evilness blossomed as I approached a light on 159th and Torrence.

"Spare any change, ma'am?"

The voice caught me off guard. I was initially in a complete daze as I sat at the light trying to think of what the fuck to do now.

The young lady looked at me as strangely as I looked at her. I was expecting to see some crack head standing at the driver's side window, and I am sure that she wasn't expecting to see a battered woman.

I chuckled. "My boyfriend. Long story," I said to explain my black eye and busted lip. "What do you need change for?"

"I'm trying to get on the bus. I lost my transfer."

"How far are you going?"

"Chicago. Southside."

"I'm headed that way. You want a ride?"

She looked skeptical at first but then shrugged her shoulders. I guess I appeared weak to her, with a beat up face and all. Cars began to honk as the red light changed to green. The young girl jogged around to the passenger side and hopped in.

I sat inside of Jimmy's car across from the forest preserve trying to figure out my next move. I really had nowhere to go now. Without any money, and now without an ID, I was stranded in this city.

However, I had a lot more options now that I had, hopefully, fixed everything.

There was mayhem all around me. Cops were everywhere. There was an ambulance pulling away. There was nothing that they could do for that girl. She was toast... literally.

As I watched cops put up the yellow tape, my heart kind of went out to that girl. I really didn't want to kill her. There was enough blood on my hands that would never wash away. But as she sat in the passenger side telling me that I should leave the nigga that beat me, it hit me; if everyone thought I was dead, I could easily get away and start all over.

When I banged her head against the passenger window, knocking her out, all I was thinking about was survival. When I tied her to that tree and set her on fire, it was purely to make sure that any DNA was burned away and that the body would be found sooner than later. I cringed when I heard her screams. I never expected her to regain consciousness. Apparently, I hadn't been successful when I choked her, after dragging her inside of the woods.

The tap on the window nearly made me piss my pants. I looked up reluctantly to see an officer. Yet, he merely waved his baton, signaling for me to move along as he shouted to the car in front of me that this area needed to be clear. He never even made eye contact with me.

I started the car with a heavy heart. This was one life that I didn't want to take, but I had no other choice. I had done so much wrong, but it wasn't in me to give up without a fight.

You didn't think that I was just going to go away that easy, did you?

"Jimmy! We've been looking all over for you."

I smiled at him as I walked into the room in the ICU unit at Ingalls Hospital. I was so happy to finally catch this son of a bitch. He had been on the run for a little over a year for the murder and attempted murder of his ex-girlfriend, Tammy Douglas.

I chuckled as I scoped out his injuries. "Damn, who fucked you up?"

Luckily, this crazy motherfucker was handcuffed to the bed. When the paramedics got the call from 9-1-1 reporting a man stabbed in his apartment, it was just my luck that it was Jimmy Straton. I guess he would have rather been apprehended than allowing himself to bleed to death.

When he spat, "Simone Campbell," I nearly lost my cool.

"Who?" Unbeknownst to him, Simone was a suspect on another murder case that I had been investigating.

"Simone Campbell. That bitch stabbed me."

He went on to tell me some fucked up ass story about him and Simone fucking with each other and getting into some kind of lover's quarrel, but I wasn't buying that shit. It all sounded and looked suspect. I knew that Simone had recently been on the run in Atlanta for months. This nigga was lying. Since Simone was out on bail, I planned to put a warrant out for her arrest to get to the bottom of this. That bitch should have never gotten bail in the first place.

"Look, I know that I'm going to jail for a long time, but I didn't kill Tammy. I know I tried to, but I didn't do it. It was Simone."

This bitch was one crazy broad, but Jimmy wasn't too sane his damn self. So, I just looked at him, assuring myself to get to the bottom of all of this when I got back to the station.

"Okay, Jimmy..."

"Seriously!"

"Even if she did, you still attempted to murder Tammy, and you've been on the run. You're going down for this Jimmy. You're going to do time. Lots of it. There is nothing you can do about it," I said with a pleased chuckle.

"What if I have information about a murder?"

I waved my hand dismissively. "I wouldn't believe any information you gave me. Of course, you would blame Tammy's murder on someone else."

He looked at me and proved me wrong. "No, not Tammy's murder... A baby's."

Epilogue

Omari

It had been three months since Simone was killed. Knowing that that bitch was gone allowed the burden to lift slowly but surely as the days passed by.

"Hello?"

"Hey, Omari."

"What's up, Eboni?"

"Nothing. Just wondering if you can pick the kids up from daycare for me. I have to work overtime."

"No problem. Bet."

I helped Eboni out a lot with Jamari and her kids. It helped keep us both grounded. She was taking classes at Malcolm X. She wanted to try to get into their X-ray tech program once enrollment opened up. For right now, she was taking prerequisites while working at a beauty shop as the receptionist and shampoo girl. As far as I was concerned, she didn't have to work. I was willing to take care of her. Though Eboni and I maintained a platonic friendship over the last few months, she and her kids were my family. But, she insisted on working; trying to be an independent woman and what not.

Once I hung up the phone, I hopped out of my ride and walked through the parking lot towards Chicago Ridge Mall. The weather was changing, and it was time to do some fall shopping. Now that I was back feeling like myself, I was ready to get some new gear and start living the life that I fought so hard to obtain for myself and Aeysha. I had done so many things for her and my daughter. They weren't here, but, instead of grieving, I wanted to live life to the fullest for them.

Just was I entered the mall, the sweetest smell came over me. I looked down and saw a woman texting on her phone, clearly not paying attention to what she was doing until she collided with me.

"Ooo, I'm sorry! I am *so* sorry."

Man, she was beautiful. Her smile was like a light, as she laughed at her own clumsiness. She made a nigga feel like somebody when she finally stared into my eyes and literally lost herself.

"It's okay, man," I told her. She was stuck a little bit, and so was I. Man, this girl was beautiful, and she was built like a racehorse. And it was something about her presence.

Just standing there with her was different. I felt comfortable and right.

It was weird…in a good way.

I was actually nervous. She obviously was hesitant to walk away. She was waiting for me to say something, and I was waiting for something smooth to come out of my mouth.

"What's your name?" she asked, taking the lead with a smile that was full of confidence.

"Omari Sutton." She laughed at the fact that I had given her my first and last name. But fuck that. This girl was something else. I wanted her to know me! "Where are you from?" Her accent caught me off guard. She spoke much more proper than chicks from the Chi.

"I'm from Chicago, but I just moved back home a few weeks ago."

Man, I couldn't believe that I was gazing at this woman like this. Mind you, yes, she had an ass the size of Texas and she was a pretty brown-skinned girl. But it was something about her smile. It was so genuine and real, much like Aeysha's.

I finally figured out how to make a complete sentence. "I'm sorry for staring, but you are so beautiful." She blushed as I asked, "Can I have your number?"

Just asking that question was so weird to me. I hadn't done that in, what felt like, years. I hadn't courted a new woman since Simone. And just the thought of that bitch made me want to avoid every woman in the world, including my own mother.

We moved to the side to exchange numbers. As I followed her, I admired the maxi dress that she was wearing. She was only about 5'4," so the long dress swept the floor as she walked. Her ass jiggled below hair that hung down her back. It definitely wasn't real. It looked like that banana boat shit that Simone always wore and that Aeysha wished I could afford back then. But it looked good.

I was happy to save *this* number into my phone. "What's your name?"

Again, she was smiling into my eyes. I did everything that I could to squint and make these gray eyes work magic on her. "Jasmine. Jasmine Mays."

to be continued...

A note to readers: Okay, so I know that *some* of you are mad that Simone is still alive. Hey, don't blame me! Blame the rest of the readers that love to hate her and didn't want to see her die just yet. I do read *some* of my reviews. Some people weren't ready for her to die, and majority ruled. I also saw that you all felt that I left some things hanging, so I had to keep her around for *juuuust* a little while longer. I also know that none of us want this craziness with Simone to be dragged out. I am keeping that in mind as I wrap up Secrets of a Side Bitch 4.

Please use #SimoneCampbell when tweeting about this book! I will be looking for it and retweeting your tweets!

Text "Jessica" to 25827 to receive text alerts when new releases from Jessica Watkins Presents go live on Amazon.com!

JESSICA'S CONTACT INFO

Facebook: http://www.facebook.com/authorjwatkins

Twitter: @authorjwatkins

Instagram: @authorjwatkins

Email: jessica@femistrypress.net

Become a published author:

Jessica Watkins Presents is currently accepting submissions for the following genres: African American Romance, Urban Fiction, Women's Fiction, and Multicultural/Interracial Romance. If you are interested in becoming an author, send a synopsis and the first three chapters to jwp.submissions@gmail.com.

Made in the USA
Las Vegas, NV
02 July 2023

74173963R10160